SWORD IN SHEATH

A novel by

ANDRE NORTON

UNICORN-STAR PRESS

A division of Laranmark, Inc   Neshkoro, Wisconsin

A UNICORN-STAR PRESS BOOK

Published by Laranmark Press

First Unicorn-Star Press Edition: January 1985

First Copyright © 1949
 Renewed 1977 by Andre Norton

ISBN: 0-910937-27-3

Reprint of 1949 Harcourt, Brace and Co. release

Printed by: Worzalla Publishing Co., 3535 Jefferson, Stevens Point, Wisconsin

Cover Illustration by Keith Ward

The author wishes to acknowledge a debt to Mr. E. M. T. Veelbehr, late of the Dutch East Indies and now of Hilversum, Holland, who furnished a wealth of material about the islands and their customs — and to Joop and Hanny Wemelsfelder of Dordrecht, Holland, for their many letters about the youth of postwar Netherlands.

CONTENTS

My son, beware even a sheathed sword,
for within the scabbard still lies the blade.

— FROM THE LOG BOOK OF DATU COOMS

Sword In Sheath

1

OPERATION LAZARUS

The tall young man with close-cropped dark red hair showing beneath the snap brim of his gray hat was pushed by the noonday crowd to the very back of the express elevator. He curled his fingers around the brass rail screwed to the wall and waited for the upward surge which always did strange things to his stomach. He'd flown the Hump and stepped into outer space over Burma and several assorted islands with practically no qualms at all, but he still felt a little unhappy on elevators.

"Twenty-fourth!"

Lawrence Kane sidled by the long pheasant tail on the feminine hat just in front of him and pushed past two much stouter members of his own sex to gain the tiled floor of the hallway. As the door clanged shut behind him he began reading the firm names lettered on the office entrances.

Smithfield Brothers — coughdrops maybe? Conway and Company, Incorporated. Safield & Wiggins — this

Sword In Sheath 7

was it.

He pushed open the door and walked into a reception room where fat chairs upholstered in wine leather were placed at precise angles on a thick gray carpet. It was very plump and satisified with itself, was that room. He decided that he liked better the stark black and white of the corridor. If it hadn't been for the cable nesting in his pocket — But he was not to be intimidated by chairs — even burgundy ones.

"Yes, sir?" A vision of great beauty materialized behind a discreet inquiry desk.

But he was able to reply in a voice which sounded steady and matter-of-fact even in his own ears.

"My name is Kane. I have an appointment — "

"Oh, yes, Mr. Kane. You are expected. If you will be kind enough to wait a few minutes. Mr. Safield is in conference — "

She indicated the circle of chairs, and he obediently made his way towards the nearest, suppressing an idiotic desire to tiptoe lest his very human foot — in its size ten-and-a-half covering — leave some disfiguring stain on the carpet.

Even after nearly five months in which he had had every opportunity to become once more thoroughly civilized, to accept beds, chairs and tables as necessities instead of exotic luxuries, he found this room a little overpowering. As he lowered himself gingerly into the soft embrace of the leather, he wondered if one dared pollute this rarefied atmosphere with the smoke of an ordinary cigarette.

Why in the world had Dick Boone ever brought him here anyway? Kane pinched the folded slip of cablegram which had summoned him halfway across the continent, an army war-bag for luggage and a very wild hope in his heart. Dead-Eye had never let him down yet. If *he* said that this was what they had been waiting for — then it was.

Lawrence Kane, ex-lieutenant O.S.S., reached for a copy of *Life* from the table at his elbow and tried to focus his thoughts as well as his eyes on the fascinating details of a steel worker's home life. But other scenes kept forming across the open pages.

Green trees, half-strangled with looped vines and thriving parasites, shot up and closed ranks in a thick wall of vegetation screening a mountain trail which was only a cut of brown, viscous mud. And the rain which never stopped drummed again in his ears, even as he was able to taste the brack of atabrine across a shriveled tongue.

The trees became shadows and were gone, vanished into the cold gray sweeps of rugged hillside where raw mountains loomed above — ragged mountains which might have been part of the ravaged landscape of the moon. A lance of wind blew down them to cut through leather and fur and spike his shivering body.

The rain forests of the dark islands, the foothills of Assam, now were as much a part of him as the nails on his fingers or the hair cropped so close to his head.

He mouthed a stick of gum, pressing out the mint flavor with his teeth. Even the memory of atabrine was enough to make a man gag. He glanced down at the crease in the gray trousers which would have been so much more comfortable had they been sun-bleached khaki. At first sight he had liked this suit, but now he didn't care for it — any more than he liked this office. For two cents, cash money, he'd get up now and walk out. Mr. Safield and his conferences could —

Kane bit hard on his gum and tossed the magazine back on the table. If this Safield didn't show soon —

But it was not Mr. Safield who pushed into the reception room. Kane's eyes widened in a disbelief which warmed into pure joy as he watched the man who had entered cross to the desk. Shifting the gum to his cheek, the ex-lieutenant pulled himself out of the chair, a crooked grin which lifted years from his brown face curling the lips of his wide mouth.

"Can it be — it's the Grand Lama himself!" he said softly. But the words carried well, and the slight figure across the room swung around, his face for once losing its habitual calm.

"Dutch! Dutch Kane!"

Kane's hand rose in a swift salute which was half the Arab salutation of hand to brow and half army courtesy. The other returned the gesture solemnly.

"What is this anyway? Old home week?"

"It looks that way. Did Dead-Eye pull you here too?"

Ex-Master Sergeant Sam Marusaki shook his head. "No. I had a telegram from old Ironjaw himself and — "

"Ironjaw!" Kane's grin was splitting his face now. "If he's in on the deal, then Dick is right. This is big!"

"What do you mean?"

"This must be the job Dick hinted that we might get a chance at — You know — " Kane suddenly felt a little foolish. Maybe he'd been on the point of saying too much, just because he was so darn glad to see Sam again. He must have it bad if just meeting one of the old outfit could set him to jawing so wildly.

Now Sam was standing there, cool as the old boy himself, lighting a smoke and looking around as if he owned the place and used it to keep ragpickers waiting in. Nothing much could ruffle Sam, though — except snakes. There was the time he'd sat down under a python's happy home tree — what had happened then had been exciting enough.

"How's the civilian?" Kane began again.

Sam pitched his match into the cup of the smoking stand. "As well as can be expected. How's the home town boy — making good?"

Kane plunged. "Plenty fed up — if you must know."

A thin plume of smoke curled from Marusaki's full nostrils. "Tell papa all about it," he suggested mildly. And his tone did it — ripped off that gray suit and pushed away the room. Kane relaxed as the wire snap went out of his nerves.

"I don't think I fit into this any more." A wave of his hand indicated his present world.

"Well, you aren't the only one, brother."

"You too?" There had been no mistaking the ring in Sam's voice.

"Yeah, me too. You aren't unique, fella. This is about my last hope." He took from his pocket a yellow slip which was as well crumpled as the one Kane carried. "My blood pressure went up a hundred points when I first read these beautiful, beautiful words. D'you think that this means back to the Army again?"

"It can mean anything. But with Dead-Eye and Iron-jaw running it — it means trouble for someone. Just now I'm not too particular who — as long as I'm allowed to play too — "

"Roger." Sam perched on the edge of the magazine table, just as he had perched on the edges of boxes and crates, the seats of jeeps, and the worn steps of time-forgotten jungle temples. Just to see Sam as casual as ever made one feel good. Kane beamed.

"Trouble for someone," Sam was musing. "Army of occupation stuff, I wonder?" His eyebrows, as thin and well-shaped as those possessed by the receptionist, moved upward. Kane shook his head.

"I don't think so. That'd go through regular channels. But Dead-Eye used to have contacts in the islands before the war. It may be something to do down there now that the late dust-up is over — "

"The late dust-up — as you so optimistically refer to it

— is still going on — unofficially," Sam pointed out. "Fighting a peace is a darn sight harder than fighting a war. You have to do it with mittens on, and, like as not, the other fellow is equipped with a flame-thrower. The islands — hmm. I wonder. If it's New Guinea or Borneo again, I'm packing waterwings. Remember the pleasures of Dead Chinaman Camp?"

"Will I ever forget them? My pet nightmare has me trying to escape from a leech and one of those elephant-sized flies at the same time. I'll take China or Burma — "

"And it might well be either," Marusaki agreed. "Well, I like chop suey. When do we push off?"

"I suppose after we learn where we're going. I only hope we *are* going. This Safield was to see me at ten — it's half-past now. You don't suppose something's gone wrong?" He shivered. To be let down now after all their dreaming —

"Mr. Kane, Mr. Marusaki." The receptionist drifted into view. "Mr. Safield will see you now. The door on the left, please."

The door on the left brought them into the kind of office which both had hitherto believed existed only in the imagination of a movie-set artist. From behind a desk which seemed half as long as a city block, a man arose with a murmur of greeting, but his companion did not stir from his chair. Instead he nodded to the newcomers curtly, as if they had met for the last time at mess that morning, instead of in India six months before.

Kane's hand half rose before he remembered their change of status. Civilians didn't have to salute even Ironjaw. But his hand still twitched as he seated himself on the chair the colonel had indicated. Colonel Archibald Thurston had that odd effect upon people. It had been rumored — and firmly believed by anyone who had ever served under his command — that even some exalted beings who were entitled to wear three and four stars on their shoulders were none too comfortable when unable to evade Ironjaw on the warpath.

Not that he appeared to be on the warpath now. Long familiarity with that craggy face, and the emotions and thoughts stowed behind it, led Kane to diagnose now that the colonel was merely interested. Which meant — his fingers curled into his palms — that Dick was right!

The man behind the desk turned to Thurston as if the colonel was expected to make introductions. And with his customary dryness he did.

"Mr. Safield, these men are Kane and Marusaki, the two of whom I spoke to you last week. They served under my command for twenty months — satisfactorily."

"Satisfactorily!" And that from Ironjaw himself! Kane was a little dazed as he waited for Safield to get down to business.

Only Safield seemed unable to do that. He was a tall man, the bones of his long and narrow head prominently outlined beneath the yellow-white skin of a man ill in either mind or body. But when he raised heavy eyelids and looked straight at Kane, the younger man shifted uneasily. He had seen that unreasoning gleam in other men's eyes, in the eyes of liberated captives of Bataan. Safield was a man who had lived with torture a long, long time.

"How well do you know the East Indies?" he asked at last.

"Which islands?" countered Sam. "There're hundreds of them and of the island groups, you know. We have served in Borneo and New Guinea."

Safield thrust back into its onyx-based holder the pen he had been fingering. "I don't know," he answered drearily. "That's the worst — I don't know!"

Thurston cut in smoothly, talking to cover Safield's breakdown.

"Marusaki is Japanese-American of the third generation. He speaks Japanese, Malay, and Chinese. He served under my command in the O.S.S. with the rank of master sergeant and was one of the men responsible for bringing to a successful conclusion Operation Lincoln — the liberation of a secret prisoner-of-war slave camp on an island in the Sulu archipelago where the Japanese had established a hidden sub base.

"Kane was a lieutenant in the O.S.S. He speaks Dutch, Malay, and some Chinese. He was second in command on Operation Lincoln — under Capt. Boone. Both of these men know something of the territory in question. You will be able to find very few Americans better suited for your purpose. I recommend them unreservedly — "

"Whew!" Kane's lips shaped the exclamation he dared not voice. Ironjaw was spreading it on thick. Why was Thurston so eager to sell them to Safield? Not for any real interest in Safield's problem — he could guess that. To Ironjaw only one thing mattered — the Job. Kane knew the old tickle of excitement between his shoulder blades. So the Job wasn't over yet — in spite of all the disbanding and mustering out!

"Yes — yes — of course." Safield pulled his attention back to the room and the men in it. "Well, gentlemen, on the recommendation of Col. Thurston I have asked you here, hoping you will see fit to undertake a mission for me. A mission which means a great deal —

"My son, my only son, Rodney Safield, served in the South Pacific with the Air Force. In the summer of 1944 he went on a bombing raid to the island of Celebes. His plane did not return."

Somewhere in the room a clock was ticking. As Kane listened to that steady beat he wondered how many times Safield must have been conscious of it too — of the minutes passing —

"There have been some cases recently of missing men

being found in the islands — located after months and even years." Thurston's crisp tone drowned out the cruel ticking. "Mr. Safield believes — "

"I believe that Rodney may still be alive — alive somewhere!" With shaking hands he pulled open a desk drawer and bundled out a map, crumpled, creased, and much marked with pencil and ink. "I've had experts advise me, men who know the islands. Here among the Moluccas, among the islands of the Banda Seas, north of Timor, are places where white men have not been, where even native traders have not touched in years. Rodney may be on one of those. Or — or you may find his grave — " He smoothed the map carefully, making a heavy business of rubbing out the wrinkles. "I'm told that some of the natives are Christian, that they have buried our men and care for the graves. But living or dead — I must know — I must know —!" He beat down upon the map with his fist, a dull tattoo which matched the deadly rhythm of the clock.

"Here!" He dragged from the drawer another mass of papers, some bearing official seals and stamps. "I have the proper credentials, letters of credit, tickets, everything you'll need to get you there — if you'll take the job."

Kane looked at Sam. It sounded crazy. On the other hand Ironjaw wanted them to do it, and Dick must have a hand in it, too, as his cable witnessed. Sam's brown eyes met the green ones of his old messmate, and in them Kane read his answer.

"All right. When do we start?" he asked for them both.

Safield was like a drowning man who had gulped air. "Col. Thruston" — he jerked his head toward Ironjaw — "will arrange the details. Please, gentlemen, if you will be good enough to excuse me — "

He stumbled out of his chair and groped his way to a door in the far corner of the room. Thurston reached over to scoop the papers into a briefcase.

A half hour later Kane and Sam were in the very utilitarian office which Col. Thurston had made his own with the same ease which had transformed numerous thatched huts into temporary Pentagons. A slight nod permitted them refuge on straight-backed chairs never intended to give aid or comfort to the normal human form, and, encouraged by this unusual amiability, Kane dared to ask a question.

"What's the score, sir?"

The colonel did not use his famous atomic glare in answer.

"You two are going into the East Indies on your own, strictly on your own." Thurston's smile was the joyless, restricted grin of a hungry shark. "You are private citizens of the United States without official standing of any sort — "

"This can prove that." Sam dug a fingernail into the discharge button on his jacket lapel. "Only maybe we're to be something else too — "

Thurston seemed to be enjoying his own thoughts, working his long bony fingers together, a gesture of pleasure which they both had reason to remember. "Not so fast, Marusaki. You will be private citizens and none of our concern. Understand? Of course, should you care to make a note of anything unusual you see during your travels — "

Kane's mouth grimaced. "Nice game. If we slip you've never heard of us. Just like that — "

Ironjaw lost his sweetness. "D'you young fools realize what's happening to us? We demobilized at a rate which almost ruined everything we'd accomplished. Green kids make up the armies of occupation — they haven't an idea in a hundred of their soft heads! The O.S.S. is gone. Our tools are out of our hands — and yet we have to sweat to keep the machine running. You're both members of the Reserve. I could have you back in uniform in an hour.

Only what use would you be to me then?"

"And I'm not returning to K.P. and the joys of post duty without a squawk you can hear from here to Washington," struck in Sam. "But what's the pitch in the Indies, sir, that you need eyes and ears down there? I can see now how Safield got permission to send us out as a private expedition — "

The colonel was busy sorting into different piles the papers he had brought from Safield's office.

"These should take you anywhere in the Indies. Our government is interested in missing flyers — there is an organization being formed with just such duties. Your trip will be considered in the nature of an experiment. And don't concentrate on young Safield alone. Here is a list of others who have vanished in the same area — You have seats booked aboard the Hawaii clipper which leaves tomorrow. From there you're to fly to Manila and report to Boone."

But Kane refused to be dismissed so easily. "What's wrong down there, sir?" he persisted.

"What's right?" countered the colonel. "The Dutch are fighting native reds in Java, all sorts of queer people are floating around. Use your eyes — and your wits — if you still have a teacupful of them left. Boone will brief you. Good day, gentlemen, and — good luck."

Outside Kane laughed. "Ironjaw can give the brush-off quicker and more neatly than any other brass I've ever met. What do you think of the set-up anyway, Sam?"

"Lloyds of London would turn down our applications at once — and they have the reputation of insuring everything and anything."

Kane's eyes narrowed. "Well, it's nice to have my worst fears confirmed so quickly. Let's go and pick out coffins, shall we? I wonder if Ironjaw will remember to send lilies?"

"Lilies? When he's never heard of us? This interview

never happened — officially."

"Just a sort of nightmare, you mean? I suppose Iron-jaw was the gristle in the hamburger I ate last night. Okay. But what are we going to do about our kits? I don't see myself coasting about the islands in this natty little gray number."

"That's been taken care of, apparently." Sam was glancing over his share of the papers. "Says so right here. We report to this address for kit and all supplies."

"Then what are we waiting for? I give you Operation — Operation Lazarus!"

Sam considered the point before he nodded agreement. "Operation Lazarus it is, Dutch."

2

"WE'RE UNOFFICIAL,
VERY, VERY UNOFFICIAL!"

"**G**lad I never said that I could decipher chicken tracks!" Kane stretched his long legs, trying to ease muscles weary from hours of walking about Manila. He curled his bare toes over the foot rail of the bed and half-dollar sized flakes of once white paint scaled off to the floor.

The rest of the small room was in keeping with the ancient bed. Above Kane's pillowed head a line of plugged bullet holes in the stained wall was a reminder of the martyrdom of Manila's last days of captivity. There was only one light, a naked bulb swinging from a black cord looped above the battered table.

And under its glare Sam was hunched over a collection of dirty papers. His brown back was bare from the neck fringe of his wavy black hair — gift of at least one Hawaiian ancestor — to where a pair of green-and-orange shorts were on duty. His skin had an oily sheen, and now and again he rubbed face and chest with a towel.

It was smotheringly hot, and somehow the dusk gathering outside the cloth-screened window made the heat thicker — more tangible. Kane mused. Was it worth the energy expended to reach for the lime drink he had left on the chair by the bed? He decided it was not — just as Sam raised his head and rubbed his eyes wearily.

"Those chicken tracks might be of importance," he answered Kane's remark of minutes before. "And men were writing books using these characters to express abstract thoughts when — "

"When my barbarian ancestors wore blue paint for Sunday best. Yeah, I've heard that one before. Only take it easy, fella, this is no climate in which to work yourself to death. You've been on that job too long. When Dead-Eye dropped those in your lap he didn't mean that they were to be translated today — "

"Didn't he? You should know our Capt. Boone better. I think he will — "

"Will what?"

From force of long habit Kane's hand whipped under the pillow beneath his head — just as Sam's went as swiftly to the gleam of steel in the waistband of his shorts. Then both relaxed as the loose-jointed man at the door came into the full light of the room, shoved Kane's legs over, and coolly sat down on the bed without waiting for an invitation from its occupant.

"Boone will what?" He repeated his question.

"Someday" — Kane was scowling — "you'll get a slug right between your eyes because you pussy-footed around where you weren't wanted, Dead-Eye."

"If you continue to keep your gun here" — Capt. Richard Boone gave the pillow a twitch to reveal a wicked and well-kept automatic — "you won't be the one to do it. And why am I greeted in such a bloodthirsty fashion anyway? Haven't you boys thrown away your cloaks and daggers yet? Fie — you are peaceable private citizens now, you know."

"Are we?" Sam was arranging his papers in two piles. "Old Ironjaw spoke a little differently on the same subject. Well, here's your dirt, Boone — at least all that I have been able to translate so far. This bright effusion on top is a poem about cherry blossoms in the early spring. The poet has a lousy sense of rhyme and a fair memory for everything he has ever heard on the subject.

"Next we have a bill of sale for five measures of rice, across the bottom of which is a comment about the state of the rice when received which will not bear repeating, not even in this low company. Then we have a quaint bit of local color — an order to one Susaki to watch someone referred to throughout as 'he', very unenlightening. Susaki is to make daily reports — "

Boone reached over and deftly plucked the paper out of Sam's grasp.

"I'll take that one. Anything else."

"Two letters from homesick soldiers." Sam shrugged. "Pretty mixed batch. What were you expecting — an expose of the late secret police?"

Boone put Susaki's instructions away in his wallet. "I don't ever expect anything from these little grab bags. I just accept thankfully what the gods may send. That all?"

"Two here I haven't had a chance to do yet. Most of these chaps write a vile hand — "

"Well, slave driver, did he pass with honors?" Kane rolled over.

"Pass — ?" murmured Boone.

"Yeah. Didn't you give him that mess of junk just to see whether the old brain was still functioning? As if you didn't have a corps of good translators right under your nose at headquarters! I wonder what sort of an exam you've cooked up to put me through. And speaking of gifts from the gods — has anyone sent us the means of getting out of this stewpot? We didn't fly halfway around the world to translate rice bills and poems about cherry blossoms. We're working men, remember? And there's going to be a question or two asked if we don't begin to deliver. Mr. Safield may be paying for our stay in this dump, but that doesn't endear it to us — "

"I'll have you know, my pampered pet" — Boone shed his cap and unbuttoned two more buttons on his damp shirt — "that there are good men and true on Leyte and elsewhere who would look upon these comfortable quarters as the height of luxury. You've been spoiled by too much stateside — "

"If this is luxury — " Kane grinned. "Oh, I know — there was a war on hereabouts. But seriously, Dead-Eye, what about a little trip south for us?"

"How would you like a voyage to the Celebes? See the strange native villages, revel in the cool sea breezes, sail romantically through the old pirate seas of the Sulu straits — "

"In what?" demanded Sam suspiciously. "A worm-eaten prau?"

"In a nice clean Dutch steamer, a pre-war freighter. She's right here in the harbor now — bound for Jolo, Manado, and points south, wherever she can pick up cargo. She's the *Sumba*, Klees van Bleeker, captain. He was carrying cargo for us during the war, knows the islands like his own hand, and may be willing to take passengers. The war wiped him out financially, all he has left is his ship."

"The department vouches for him?" queried Sam.

But Boone refused to answer that leading question. "Judge him for yourself. He's co-operative enough, a nice guy. You'll find him in town now, down at the old Casa Blanca. Part of the roof's still on the lobby, so it's in business again."

"And do we let van Bleeker into our little secrets?" asked Kane lazily.

Again Boone did not answer directly. He took out a cigarette and turned it around in his fingers, studying the white tube as if he had never seen one of those very interesting objects before.

"I don't know," he began slowly, "how much you've learned about the situation out here. Oh, we've supposedly liberated the islands and are in charge in Japan. But there's a civil war in China which may set off the powder barrel again, a revolt in Java which won't be ended in a hurry — if ever — and all sorts of dirty business afoot throughout the Indies. This is the proper time and place for interested people to try to gum up the works wherever they can. You've heard of the Nazi 'Werewolves', of the various bands of Japanese holdout troops which we come across now and again — well, we're not getting all of them — not by a long sight!

"There were German subs in these waters which we haven't found yet — among other small mysteries. And some men are clever enough to go to ground and stay there until they are forgotten. We can't go over hundreds of islands with fine-toothed combs! It'll be years before our clean-up drive is over — if it ever is. And every holdout we miss will be a festering sore.

"Just suppose some clever men — mind you, I'm not naming names — should undertake to organize little pockets of native agitators, holdout troops, ex-Nazis, and the like, on out-of-the-way islands. Keep them alive and going with supplies and use them to build up a skeleton force. If we didn't find out in time — it might be December Seventh all over again some fine day.

"Now you're going to head straight into the biggest danger point — the Indies. There're hundreds of islands down there, some of which white men have never explored, some which Europeans haven't visited in years

— officially. Even the Japs didn't seem to pay much attention to them — then. But now you might be able to discover some very odd colonies taking root on them. A Nazi on the run or a Jap holdout has nothing to lose now if he changes masters. He'll eat regular, get ammunition for his guns, and can squat down to prepare for the big day when he can settle a few scores again. And if you do find anyting of that sort — "

"We promise faithfully to tell you all about it." Sam held a light to Boone's cigarette. "Emulating the estimable Susaki, we shall inform you at the proper intervals of our progress. I only hope that we are not expected to be boy heroes. I am neither Terry Lee nor Steve Canyon, you understand. Mouse blood courses sluggishly through my veins."

Kane snorted. "Sure, we know all about you and your mouse blood! All right, Dead-Eye, we'll double as your gumshoe boys. But to whom do we report any nefarious dealings which we may uncover — or are you about to present us with a new invisible walkie-talkie to conceal about our persons that we may use to summon the fleet at the proper moment? A couple of those atomic blasters used by the best science-fiction heroes would be nice too — and maybe a coat of mail apiece — these island boys carry knives."

"You will be contacted at the right time. Keep in touch with van Bleeker, his knowledge of the Indies and their people will be invaluable. And if you get in a jam — " He hesitated, and Sam grinned, wryly.

"We do NOT send for the Marines. Yes, Ironjaw made that point clear. We're unoffical, very, very, unoffical!"

Boone nodded. "That's the way it has to be — sorry. If you want to walk out — no hard feelings."

Kane's toes moved across the bed rail and more paint flakes went to the floor. "Oh, we're sitting in. I wanted a job like this one. After all, ending as hut decoration for a head-hunter is just what I have always fancied. And since Burma, life in the States seems a little too tame. I don't know how Sam feels about it — "

"He endorses your sentiments heartily. Having worn a cloak and brandished a dagger successfully — I find that I no longer have a taste for the simple life. Yes, Capitan Boone, thank you kindly — we're island bound. Now is the time for you to rise and survey us proudly as, with simple and moving dignity, you utter those classic and tear-compelling words, 'Good luck, men'."

"Just for that crack, I will. Good luck. You'll probably need all of that commodity you can get. Now you'd better see van Bleeker as soon as you can. The *Sumba* sails when she has finished loading trade goods — "

"Okay, tall brass. We hear and obey. I hope the ship has a decent cook. Good-bye, mug, we'll be seeing you — "

Boone blew a long plume of smoke. "I'll hold you to that promise, smart boy. Three months from now you'd better come around again or else!" With a wave of his hand he left.

"Or else," mused Sam. "It seems to me that there are chances for a great many or-elses in this pleasant little excursion. Dressing?" He watched Kane pull on a shirt. "Aren't you being a little rash — that's next to your last clean shirt, and you don't have to be beautiful for me — I'm not proud."

"You heard our orders. We go to the Casa Blanca and find this van Bleeker before he pulls out and leaves us sitting on the beach with not a ship in sight. Come on — rise and shine."

With a groan Sam kicked off loose slippers and reached for his shoes while his roommate decided against the formality of a necktie.

After the unshaded light of their room the dusk outside was soft and soothing to the eyes. Manila had come to life — a broken life with the ugly scars of burns and unforgettable wounds to warp what had once been the heart of a free country. But it was free once more, and that was all which seemed to matter to its inhabitants. Tonight the streets were crowded, and there was actually laughter to be heard now and then. Manila was on the way back.

The Casa Blanca had once been a luxury hotel. And now, as Boone had pointed out, because it still boasted part of a roof, it was in business again, prized by those lucky enough to find shelter within its bullet-pocked walls. Kane inquired at the desk for van Bleeker and had pointed out to him a slender man in the spotless white of a ship's officer who sat alone at a table in the restaurant corner of the lobby.

"Capt. van Bleeker?"

The man who might have been in his middle forties raised his eyes politely to Kane's. The weathered skin of a seaman was a mask beneath a thick tangle of what once might have been blond hair. Now sun-bleached to silver white, that mop was as startling as the two very fair eyebrows against his dark skin.

"I am Capt. van Bleeker, yes. You will sit please, gentlemen." He waved an invitation, and the Americans slid into the vacant chairs at the table while the master of the *Sumba* sipped his drink and waited for them to state their business.

"I am Lawrence Kane ,and this is Sam Marusaki. We're interested in taking passage down to the Moluccas, and we heard that you are sailing for there — "

"Perhaps," returned van Bleeker tranquilly. "The *Sumba* is an island trader; she sails where she can find a cargo. And she is no passenger ship, gentlemen."

"We understand that, Captain. But Capt. Boone of the United States Army suggested that we speak to you.

We're trying to find a man who disappeared over the Banda or Arafura Seas, the pilot of a bomber reported missing somewhere between Timor Laotet and the Soelas."

Van Bleeker smiled politely. "That is something of a wide territory to cover. If you do not have any definite clues — " He shrugged and raised his glass.

"But you are bound for that section, aren't you?" persisted Sam.

"I sail for Jolo in the Sulus and then to Manado in Celebes — from there" — he shook his head — "it may be anywhere. You understand, I am a pioneer in reestablishing trade. I must go where I can find profit. During the occupation our business with the islands was wiped out. We must begin again. And southward there are hundreds of islands — your task is a formidable one, gentlemen. I do not envy you."

"We can avoid the larger islands and those which have been visited recently by our forces. Our man would have been found if he were on one of those. But there are small islands — "

"True. And some of them are not even on any map — totally unknown except to native turtle fishermen. For a man to be lost thereabouts is not impossible. There is, for example, the classic case of the men of Kissar — "

"Kissar?"

"Yes. A famous case, as unusual as that of the *Bounty* men who settle Pitcairn's Island. When the armies of the French Revolution overran the Netherlands, our island empire was cut off from the motherland for years. The British took over Sumatra and Java and those of the larger islands whose trade made it worth their while to control. But they did not bother to visit the smaller outposts on some of the little islands. Among those so disregarded was Kissar, which has no anchorage and was not a regular port of call. Left to its own devices upon

Kissar was a colony of Netherlanders, soldiers and merchants — some with European wives. For fifty years or more Kissar was off the maps of the world.

"Then one day a coasting ship, much like my *Sumba*, sent a party ashore there — perhaps she needed water — perhaps her master was of a curious turn of mind. There the crew discovered a colony still in being, a colony whose members lived, dressed and spoke as Coast-Malays, but who were as Dutch in blood as Amsterdam itself. And to this day the men of Kissar continue to live as aliens to their blood — to all purposes they are island natives. What has happened before may well happen again. I would not say that your man cannot be found.

"But the *Sumba* goes only for trade, where she may find cargo. If you sail with me you must abide by my decision as to route. If you discover a clue and wish to trace it to its source — the source being an island where the *Sumba* does not touch — well, that will then be your problem, not mine."

"Fair enough," Kane agreed. "Then you will take us?"

"Before the war the *Sumba* carried a few passengers at times. I have two extra cabins. One of them is yours, if you wish, since Capt. Boone sent you to me. I have the pleasure of his acquaintance."

"Do you have any other passengers?" asked Sam.

"One. A countryman of mine, who, before 1941, had extensive business interests in the Indies. And now, if you wish to embark on the *Sumba*, I would suggest that you get your gear aboard tonight. We sail early in the morning."

"What is the passage charge?" Kane wanted to know.

Van Bleeker shook his head. "Since you do not know as yet how far you will travel, I cannot say. Let us settle that when you leave the *Sumba*. Will that be satisfactory?"

"Certainly. You sail very early?"

"Yes. I would advise being aboard by midnight. I trust you will find the *Sumba* a pleasant ship. Until we meet again, gentlemen." He raised his glass in a half-toast as Kane and Marusaki got to their feet.

But Sam was frowning as they walked out to the street. "Our worthy captain is not quite the simple soul he would have us believe him. And what about this other passenger — who or what is he?"

"Boone steered us to the *Sumba*, and Dead-Eye knows his stuff. You think that there's something wrong with the set-up?"

"A little too smooth. Van Bleeker is so obliging that one could almost believe our passage had been all arranged before we ever showed up."

"That may be Dead-Eye's little present to us."

"I certainly hope so. We'll be stuck on this tub a good long time, and lots of queer things could happen to us without any awkward questions being asked later."

"You don't trust van Bleeker?"

"I don't know. He's sea-shipped cream. But I'd hate to be on the other side of any bargains he's making. Oh, blast! Maybe I'm just off my feed. Too much paper work in that oven this afternoon. Let's get our stuff and pull out of this swelter. There may be a breeze hanging around down on the bay."

When Kane opened the door of their room and felt about for the light cord he allowed himself a slightly annoyed comment.

"You *are* off the beam. Forgetting to lock the door — "

"What d'you mean — forgetting to lock the door! I tried it, and it was tight enough when — "

"I think then" — the light snapped on, Kane's mouth became a thin line, his eyes burned green — "we've had a visitor. Pity he didn't stay to meet us. Untidy creature, wasn't he?"

Sheets and pillows had been pulled from the bed and

lay in a muddle on the floor. From the sides of both pillows feathers gushed through rents in the ticking. Their kit bags had been emptied by the simple method of turning them upsdie down upon the mattress of the denuded bed. After that the linings had been ripped from their interiors. There was not a lid left on any box, and Sam gave a soft, furious exclamation as he stooped to pick up a tube of shaving cream, the contents of which had been squeezed out across the front of a clean shirt.

"Somebody wanted something and wanted it bad." Kane started sorting through his maltreated wardrobe. "I wonder what they thought we were transporting — crown jewels?" He found a neat coil of tooth paste on one pajama leg and swore — hurling the flat tube across the room.

"No hotel theif did all this," began Sam.

"Don't you suppose I've guessed that?" snapped Kane. "This guy — or guys — was hunting for something special. Only it would be kind of interesting to know what it was we are supposed to be carrying."

"They weren't after these anyway." Sam picked two papers out of the general mess. "These are Boone's — "

"No. They must have thought we carried something from the States. See, that package over there — the one of tropical slacks we bought today? It isn't even open. This smacks of the good old days before the war was over — "

"What d'you mean — the good old days? Look at this room!"

"Atom bomb number four. Well, let's shovel this mess into transportable shape and shove off. They've done their worst — "

"Have they? What if they are now convinced that we must be carrying this mytserious treasure on us — ?"

"You always have the most charming ideas. Shall we ask Boone for an escort down to the *Sumba*? After all it is to his advantage that we arrive on board in one piece and reasonably undamaged."

"Maybe we'd better not noise our shame aloud. But I do suggest that we look behind us now and then and avoid dark alleys. I'd like to get my hands on the fun merchant who did this!" Sam held up a pair of shorts patterned with a combination of ink and sun lotion. "I'd feed him to Ironjaw for breakfast!"

"Cloak and dagger boys — yeah!" Kane licked his fingers absentmindedly, then spat shaving cream in wry-mouthed disgust. "Brother, this was one time when we were caught off base!"

3

THE GENTLEMAN FROM ROTTERDAM

"**T**he Mijnheer will drink?"

Kane opened his eyes upon a curiously unstable world. A brown-skinned, white-coated man stood by the bunk as steady as a mile post, balancing within easy reaching distance a tray on which stood a glass, its sides beaded with moisture. Through the open cabin door came a suggestion of breeze.

Rubbing sleep-sanded eyes Kane hitched out of the lower bunk and leaned forward into the none too roomy center section where piles of luggage made an obstacle course of the small quarters. He accepted the glass and found that he was sipping iced water. After a long gulp he got to his feet and raised a hand to prod Sam into wakefulness.

The hand remained poised in mid-air because Sam wasn't alone in the upper bunk to which the flip of a coin the night before had exiled him.

Snug on the pillow beside the black head was a brown one, smaller and much neater. Thin slits of aquamarine eyes regarded Kane without much interest and a red tongue pointed contemptuously in his general direction as narrow jaws gaped wide in a yawn.

"What the — !"

Sam accepted that exclamation as his cue to roll over, roll over and face his bunkmate — apparently for the first time. His head jerked up and thumped against the ceiling. But his companion was already withdrawing gracefully. Brown legs and cream body and, last of all, a seal brown tail flowed away as the stowaway gained the top of a neighboring box, then the floor. Without so much as a glance the visitor slid out of the door and out of their sight. Kane took the second glass from the tray and handed it to Sam.

"Who's your friend?"

"I wouldn't know." Sam swung down from his perch, accepted the ice water and sat rubbing his forehead. "I'll swear it wasn't there when I crawled in last night."

"Do the mijnheeren wish anything?"

The Malay steward still hovered by the door.

"Where did that cat come from?"

"It is the cat of the ship, mijnheeren. She does not make friends easily — "

Kane laughed. "So we would guess. What is your irresistible power over women, Sam?"

"I have none that I know of. And that flea hotel better keep out of my bed in the future if it knows what is good for it!"

"Breakfast in the officers' mess in one hour, mijnheeren. Do you wish now your morning coffee?"

"Sure. Only don't bring the lady back with you."

Kane set out his shaving kit. "I think I'm going to enjoy this trip," he observed.

"Of course. Only next time the cat can sleep with you. Where did I put my toothbrush? Since our visitor back in

Manila had his way with the baggage I can't find anything. Let's make it snappy. That suggestion about breakfast hit the spot — I wonder if we dare dream of ham and eggs — "

But even prodded by appetite they weren't the first to visit the wardroom that morning. Just at the door they almost collided with a stout little man well swathed in oily dungarees at least one size too large for him. A battered officer's cap covered only the back of a large head where pinkish-sandy hair was as thick as a furry pelt. He was picking his teeth and regarding both the *Sumba* and the morning with a benevolent and proprietary air.

" 'Lo," he greeted the Americans happily with an accent which was improbaby enough that of River Bend, Iowa. "Grand day, ain't it?"

"Sure is," Kane agreed.

"You two from th' States?"

"Yes."

"Kinda nice t' hear that. Not that th' Dutchies ain't good fellas — " He was fully in earnest now. "Don't ever let any guy say they ain't. I'd sign on with th' old man if I knew it t' be a fact he was bound straight fer Davy Jones' boneyard! He's th' goods, all right, all right. But I ain't bin home in ten years now. An' Statesides talk is good t' listen t'. What's it like over there now?"

"Well, different than before the war," began Kane.

"Maybe, maybe. Well, you can't have a clean boiler 'less you chip it. An' we've jus' had us a mighty big war, a mighty big one. Say, son, I didn't catch your names now — "

"I'm Lawrence Kane, and this is Sam Marusaki."

"Kane an' Marusaki. As I said before, I'm mighty glad to meet you boys." He shook hands with a vigorous pump. "I'm Washington Bridger — my old man give me a mighty big name t' live up t'. I'm chief o' th' *Sumba*. Bin in her ever since Capt. van Bleeker had me fished out o' th' water after th' battle fer th' Straits. Was in th' Carrie O., an' she got one right in her middle — went down 'fore we knew what really hit us. But, land alive, she waren't a patch on th' Sumba — so I got th' best o' that bargin. Bit o' good luck longside th' bad that time.

"An' now th' old man is goin' back t' th' island trade. Money in that jus' waitin' fer some guy t' pick it up. But — here I am — keepin' you boys from chow. Git in, git in, an' tell Chung Wei if he don't treat you right, he'll hear from me — he certainly will!"

Either the slap of that square hand or the breeze of that frog-voice blew them forward to face a row of chairs bolted to the floor before a long table. Seated at the head of the board was van Bleeker, with a stranger in open-collared shirt and slacks beside him.

"Good morning, gentlemen, I trust you rested well. We are not a regular passenger ship so you must excuse any discomfort — "

Kane laughed. "I'll be willing to bet that your brand of coffee isn't served aboard many passenger ships!"

Van Bleeker relaxed a measure of his formality. "You recognize it?"

"By name, no. But it's been a long time since I've tasted its equal."

"Yes, it cannot be found many places. It is a very old blend, best known in the Indies. But I am forgetting manners. Please excuse my rudeness in not at once introducing fellow travelers. This is my good friend the Jonkheer Lorens van Norreys from Rotterdam. And here, van Norreys, you see Mr. Lawrence Kane and Mr. Sam Marusaki from the United States — "

But Kane was gaping in a sort of wild-eyed amazement at the tall and almost painfully thin young man who had risen politely to greet them. The American was vainly trying to trace in that face, where lines and hollow now made a sober mask, some resemblance to a photograph he had treasured for years. Only the eyes, blue-gray and very alive, and the waves of crisp, yellow hair were the same.

"You're dead!" Kane blurted out.

The man from Rotterdam chuckled, and the cruel lines about his mouth were partly smoothed away by a smile of real amusement.

"And so, my dear friend, are you!"

"But they said — After your letters stopped I tried to reach you through the Red Cross — " persisted the American. "I wrote for two years, and every letter came back."

"As did the two I sent you in the spring of '45 when I was permitted to come to life again."

"The spring of '45. But that was when we were on Operation Lincoln — a hush-hush job. Lord, Lorens, what has happened to you?"

"I do not understand." Van Bleeker looked from one to the other. "Can it be that you are already friends of long standing?"

"Friends that never saw each other in the flesh before," Lorens van Norreys explained. "Our friendship was a paper one, but nonetheless real for that. We wrote regularly for several years before the war and were most ardent correspondents before I joined the Underground. After that it was much better for all to believe that Lorens van Norreys was truly dead — and so he was — very effectively, it now appears. It is indeed a strange trick of fortune which brings us two aboard the *Sumba* thus. Old Klaas would have said that it had been written so at our birth — "

"Klaas — that half-Malay follower of your grandfather — " Kane remembered. "Is he with you now?"

Van Norreys made a curious little gesture. "Klaas, like so many other worthy ones, is gone."

All the other questions which had been on Kane's tongue got no further. But Lorens smiled again.

"Sit down," he suggested, "and let me help you to some of this very excellent fruit. We have days of voyaging before us in which to catch up on ancient history. But first — tell me what brings you to the *Sumba* — to my great good luck!"

"A man hunt." Kane outlined the Safield story. "And now — what are you doing here?"

"Nothing so romantic — merely trying to open again the House of Norreys. For three hundred years we have bought jewels in these islands to resell in the world. Now I am attempting to pick up the scattered pieces of what was once a flourishing business. Being the last of the Norreys line I must be buyer, designer, and perhaps goldsmith all in one. But that is how my ancestors started the House, and we can do it again!"

"The last of the Norreys — but what of your cousin Piet — "

"Piet was a flyer — remember. And as a flyer he went to Arnhem. He did not return. Now it is left to me to prove that my grandfather's blood is not altogether lost in my veins. So I came here to the Indies to buy enough jewels to start work again. Maybe within a year or two you shall be able to see our mark on a ring or a necklace — if I am lucky."

"Jewel buying!" Sam repeated, regarding the young Netherlander with the same round-eyed wonder he would have shown had the other declared he was hunting for dragons.

"Yes. Pearls, black coral, minor stones. Whatever has been overlooked by the looters during the past few years. I have designs here, ready and waiting" — he touched his forehead with the tip of an artist's finger — "but I need the raw materials with which to bring them to life. Some of my grandfather's agents are still in trade, and with a few of them the House of Norreys still possesses a favorable balance — which I am now attempting to collect. Not in the least an adventurous or exciting occupation, believe me."

"Mijnheer Captain!"

The Eurasian second officer of the *Sumba* burst through the door and crowded past the tray-laden Chinese steward.

"The hatch, Captain — "

"And what is the matter with the hatch?" But van Bleeker was already on his feet and moving.

"It is bewitched, Captain!"

"What? What foolishness are you bleating now, Felder?"

"The truth only, sir. Come and see!"

Not only the captain but his passengers too crossed decks and climbed down ladders to the large amidships hatch. Ringing it was a crowd of native seamen who were standing there silently, just staring at what Kane first thought to be a crooked billet of wood fastened in some way to the canvas cover of the hatch.

Van Bleeker stopped short a foot or so away from the thing and squatted down to examine it closely. But he made no move to touch it. The seamen retreated as the others came up so that Kane was able to see that the object was really a crudely carved staff or cane which had been hacked from a misshapen sapling or a giant root. It was fastened to the hatch cover by a kind of net of fine black strands, the ends of which appeared to be glued to the coarse canvas.

Kane reached out an exploring finger, but Lorens jerked at his wrist.

"If you touch that," the Netherlander warned, "no man aboard the *Sumba* will come near you again."

"But what in the world is it?" demanded the bewildered American. "Looks like a cane to me."

"That is what it is — a cane, or rather a staff. Only it is a wizard's staff, the kind carried by a black magician. And who knows how many men's souls are imprisoned in it?" Lorens' voice was as serious as his frowning face. "That net holding it is knotted of human hair, which means it is under a powerful spell. No one but a priest can release it — and he only after the proper ceremonies. I wonder who would dare to put it — "

Van Bleeker was on his feet again, turning slowly to study each face in the awed ring about the hatch. "That is just what I am asking now," he interrupted. "Baka!" He singled out the man wearing the green turban of a Hadji. "From whence came this strange and devilish thing?"

"Who knows, Tuan Captain? Ali did sight it when going on watch. It is evil, very evil — "

"Baka, answer me now by your faith — do we carry on board a Guru?"

The man shivered at van Bleeker's open reference to one of those mediums who have dealings — and mostly unclean dealings — with spirits.

"Tuan Bezar!" His voice became a wail of open misery and fright. "Tuan Bezar, we are your men, long have we followed where you led, you knowing all of us — our good deeds and our bad. There is no Guru amongst us. Some ghost or devil has done this thing."

Van Bleeker combed his hair with nervous fingers. "Very well. Now shall we who are not of your blood or prey to your ghosts cover this abomination without touching it. And when we come into Jolo, you shall bring a priest to cleanse the *Sumba*. Hassan, you go to the cabin and get the cloth which lies upon the table there. We shall need also a hammer and nails."

Baka's relief was plain. "Tuan Bezar, those are the words of a wise man. It shall be done even as you have ordered."

With the help of Kane, Marasuki, and Lorens, van

Bleeker stretched the large cotton square over the netted staff, all of them avoiding the contamination of direct contact with it. Then the cloth was nailed down, and when the last nailhead was pounded flat Lorens pulled a pencil from his pocket and began to draw about the outer edge of the square a series of crosses.

"What does the Tuan Muda now, Captain?" asked Baka, daring, now that the evil was safely hidden, to come to the edge of the hatch.

"He puts upon the cloth the mystic sign of our own belief so that good may guard against evil — "

"That too is a good thought, Tuan Bezar. Is it permitted that we do likewise? Then the ghost which put it here cannot come to trouble us again. Indeed, it is a most excellent thought — "

He turned to his fellows at van Bleeker's nod of agreement and began an excited speech, but the captain beckoned to the passengers.

"That was a good idea, van Norreys, it will occupy their minds for a time. Which will give us a chance to do a little witch hunting. Better get your arms," he said to the Americans.

"You need our help?"

"If you care to give it. I'll take oath that no one of my men put that thing in place. They've all been with me for years, and if a man dabbles in that sort of nastiness he can't or won't make a secret of it for long. That wsn't there before we sailed from Manila; it must have been put in place before the watch was changed. Therefore — "

"You have a stowaway?" suggested Sam.

"If I have, I'll soon rout him out!" promised the captain. "That staff could have wrecked us. The crew would have jumped ship at Jolo if any one of us had willfully or accidentally touched it. As it is, it'll cost me enough to have the *Sumba* ritually cleansed. And, if I don't, no native will come aboard her! Somebody means trouble — bad trouble!"

Sam and Kane broke out the Reisings, inserting the twenty-cartridge clips with the ease of long practice. With a proved range of three hundred to six hundred yards, the small submachine guns would be raw murder in the close confines of the *Sumba*. No dealer in ghosts would care to try and outface them. Balancing the seven-pound weight easily across their forearms and hips the two Americans joined van Bleeker and Lorens on the bridge.

The Netherlanders eyed the Reisings with respect and some envy. Lorens had a Luger and the captain a Smith and Wesson.

"Where do we begin?" Sam wanted to know.

"At the bottom and work up. I have given the officers their orders to hold anyone or anything we manage to flush in our drive. Are we ready?"

For the next hour Kane and Sam learned more about the interior of a freighter than they had ever believed it possible to know. No hole was too cramped or too dark to admit van Bleeker's task force. But they started nothing except a rat or two. Even the small black copra bugs which were supposed to be a permanent fixture on island steamers were not to be seen. If there was a Guru on board he had the very useful knack of becoming invisible at will.

When they came out again on the deck van Bleeker's eyes were narrow, and the line of his jaw showed a stern set.

"I don't like it. Unless he has gone into the water there is no stowaway on board. Then who — " He glanced at the white patch on the hatch. There were other symbols scrawled upon it now and a variety of queer objects tied to the nailheads at the four corners. Apparently the crew had contributed most of their lucky pieces to the good cause of holding down the devil.

"Are you sure, Chief, that no one got past here?" Van Bleeker turned back to Bridger.

"Nary a one, Ca'n. Lady came 'long an' I popped her into th' radio cabin t' be outta th' way. Didn't want nobody t' use her for a target an' Sparks likes cats — "

"But it is impossible!" the captain snapped. "A man can't vanish into thin air, I tell you!"

"Maybe he ain't aboard any more." The chief hitched a sagging gunbelt to an easier rest across his paunch.

"If he went overboard, he's no concern of ours. And I hope that is just what happened to him. Well, gentlemen, it seems our hunt is over. Only I will ask all of you to keep watch for anything which seems to you to be out of the ordinary. I do not like this — I do not like it one little bit."

"What do you think?" Kane demanded when he and Sam reached their own cabin.

"I'd swear that there wasn't a stowaway. Only — "

"Only what?"

"Well, I agree with van Bleeker. I don't like the set-up. If someone is hiding out on board, he's darned slick about it — as slick as if he knows the ship extra well. Someone who did that could have kept one step ahead of us this morning and beaten us in the end. That's just a guess, of course. But it's plain someone wants to gum the works and gum them good. Maybe because we're on board — "

"What!"

"Have you forgotten our visitor in Manila? Suppose we'd found that staff first and touched it. We probably would if we hadn't been warned. Van Bleeker would have pitched us off in Jolo. He couldn't afford to keep us on board after that. And what native would have had dealings with us when the story spread that we'd meddled with a taboo? You know what the bamboo telegraph is — "

"I don't know. That's leaving a lot to just plain chance. How would this Guru, or whatever he is, know that we would be the ones to find the thing?"

"Well, anyway around it makes trouble for the *Sumba*, slows her up. Van Bleeker will have to go through this ceremony to get rid of the curse — and even after that it will be easy for some bright boy to hint around that maybe all the bad luck hasn't left us. I'll bet that that comforting thought is riding van Bleeker right now. And just how much trade will he have if a tale like that gets out? No, the guy who planted that devil-infested hunk of tree on the hatch knew what he was doing — and it was a very smart idea. Only — we'll have to find out why it was so smart and who had it."

"And how are we going to do that, my bright little man?"

"We might consult tea leaves or — "

But a pillow in the face stopped that pure flow of reason — very effectively.

4

ABDUL HAKROUN,
MERCHANT-PIRATE

"**W**elcome to Jolo, once the capital of a pirate empire, ancient seat of the Moro sultans, frontier post of the Sulu Sea — "

Kane pinched his nose. "What a smell! There's something dead around here — maybe a whale."

Sam, his guide's harangue so rudely interrupted, sniffed once and reached for a handkerchief.

The three passengers from the *Sumba* stood on the Chinese pier of Jolo, a structure which was really a wide street extending some distance into the sea. It was a jumble of odorous nipa-thatched huts, a shabby and disintegrating tenement district. From the left, where the Moro village perched on high stilts, the mud flats, left slimy and bare by the tide's retreat, added other smells to the already great accumulation cast off by the town. Somewhere inland were the broken walls of the old Spanish city, held for generations as a fort against those unsubdued fighting pirates who hurled the name of

'Moro' as a ferocious challenge to all comers. There one could find the two-story wooden houses which had been planned and built under European direction. But it was to the native nipa huts that Lorens turned now.

"Ah, here we have the tienda of one Lao Keh-Min, junk shop extraordinary, I would say." Sam studied the characters painted in gold down a strip of scarlet cloth which fluttered beside an uncurtained doorway.

"Come and see his brand of 'junk'," suggested Lorens.

They ducked the low lintel and came into a dusk which set them blinking before they were able to identify any of the queer assortment of goods heaped around the walls. A small, spider-thin gnome crawled out of the clutter and began a weird singsong which only Lorens seemed able to understand.

While Kane picked out of the general mess an old portable phonograph, an empty bird cage, and a practically new bicycle, the Netherlander interrupted the salesman sharply.

"It is the Tuan van Norreys who speaks. May I have word with the most honorable Lao?"

The spider scuttled off. And after a long moment another man, his decent merchant's robe of dull blue silk whispering as he moved, came out of the inner quarters. With the calm arrogance of one accustomed to absolute authority in his own domain, he eyed the three. Kane he dismissed with a single glance, Sam he studied a moment longer, but when his eys reached Lorens' worn face and too-thin person, they narrowed. Then he bowed, his hands politely hidden within his sleeves.

"You will excuse please" — his English was without accent — "this most miserable and rude welcome. Rumor has spoken lies again. I see that the House of Norreys is not dead. Enter, if you will be so kind, this uncomfortable and barren room of my own. There is doubtless much to be said."

Lao guided them through a narrow passageway walled with a patchwork of rotting boards, into a room which was as bare as the outer chamber was cluttered. Straight-backed, hard-seated chairs stood in stiff rows around the wall, and a cream-colored matting was soft under foot. When they were seated Lao clapped his hands, and the spider man trotted in to hand around tea bowls. Kane rubbed his fingers appreciatively over the one he had taken. It was of a clear, rich turquoise shade with a surface of fine satin.

Surprisingly it was Lao who brushed aside the usual formal compliments to say directly, "Since the honorable and high-born Jonkheer van Norreys has joined his ancestors, is it your desire to carry on the dealings of his gem-buying House, young lord?"

"It is. For many years did I learn from my grandfather such wisdom as was within my feeble power to absorb. Now I would carry on, though I cannot achieve his greatness — "

"That is so. He was such a one as is seldom born in any land. We who knew him were honored by his regard. But I have now on hand several pieces such as even he would have deigned to examine. Have I your permission to display these unworthy bits which I have gleaned?"

Lorens showed no undue eagerness to see Lao's offerings, but a second clap of his master's hands brought the misshapen servant back into the room lugging a small teakwood table which he set down before the Netherlander. Then he dragged out a box which Lao unlocked.

A square of white silk was unfolded on the dull black of the teak before Lao lifted from the chest a long narrow bundle wrapped in dull brocade. As carefully as if he were dealing with a time bomb the Chinese merchant plucked off the coverings and placed the glittering thing they concealed on the silk-covered table.

Sword In Sheath   47

Even Lorens' breath came unevenly from between half-open lips when he caught full sight of the treasure. And Sam did not try to stop an exclamation of wonder.

A four-inch skeleton of a lizard, perfect to the last tiny bone lay there — but it was not ivory or dull white — it was afire with blue and red, green and yellow — it was an opal!

"Carved from opal?" Kane asked.

"No. It is an opal itself." Lorens leaned forward but he did not venture to touch. "There was one like this found once before — in Australia back in 1909. It is in a museum now. But here in the Orient such a find is priceless. As well you know, Lao." He turned almost accusingly to the Chinese. "Perhaps one of the Rajahs of India might be able to pay your price — Norreys cannot."

Lao smiled. "Truly a great find. It was brought to me by a man once very rich. The war had ruined him. He sold it — for all the cash I could raise and borrow. Oh, he knew its value, even as you and I do. But who am I to approach the great ones? I have no big name, no honor among the lords of India. They would say that I had stolen it, and maybe I would find the law held against me. No, if Norreys does not wish to buy it, then I wish the House to act for me in this matter, bringing buyer and seller together."

"There must be proof of its origin," warned the Netherlander.

"That I know, and I am prepared to give it. This, too, was found in Australia, even as was that other you mentioned. But it was found in the early days before those of your race were interested in such gems. It was brought to Batavia by its discoverer who was one of those convicts escaping from the English colonies. He sold it for bread to a Rajah who sent it north as part of the bride gift of his daughter who sailed to marry a Malay princeling. That ship was captured by the pirates of the Straits, and the jewel came into the hands of the Sultan. One of his descendants gave it as a mark of favor to Datu Cooms — "

"Cooms! But he's been dead for thirty years or more."

"Yes, dead without a son to follow him. But he left much of his treasure to one of his captains, and it was from that man that I bought the wonder. He had it by right — "

"Did he?" Lorens' eyebrows rose quizzically. "It's true that Cooms had no heir, but it is also true that his island palace was sacked as soon as his men knew that the old man was truly dead. Well, I suppose your captain had as good a right to it as any. So you want Norreys to find a customer for you?"

"If possible. See, I have made preparation in such hope." He took from the chest an envelope of reptile skin and opened it to display a set of clear photographs, one full-size color drawing of the opal lizard, and a page of figures. "Here is all there is to be known, pictures, size, weight, history. Will the House of Norreys act for me?"

Lorens shuffled through the papers and regarded the opal lizard thoughtfully. "I can promise no sure sale — "

"Who can in this world? But if Norreys will accept the commission, then am I sure of fair dealing."

"All right, Lao, I'll do my best for you."

The Chinese showed no elation. He rewrapped his treasure in its covering, and having put it aside, he set before van Norreys three bracelets intricately fashioned of silver and set with stones which Kane was unable to identify even when Lorens handed him one of the pieces to examine.

"Your price?" And Netherlander and Chinese fell to bargaining.

Kane turned to Sam. "What is this, anyway?"

The Nisei squinted at the setting and tried it with his thumbnail. "Black coral — peculiar to these waters. Odd-looking stuff, isn't it? But, boy, that skeleton —

that's really something! Bet a fortune will change hands over that! Like to have it myself if I could afford that sort of a paperweight."

"Safield might. Wonder if Lao could give us a tip on the lower islands. Wait until Lorens gets through with his shopping, and we'll ask."

But when questioned the Chinese could give them no news.

"It is true that a man might be cast away on some forgotten island and never be found again. Many times has it happened, and nowadays there is much confusion in those seas. But I have heard nothing from those who come to trade, nothing which might be of assistance to you. Trade — " his attention flickered from Kane to Lorens — "trade has not been so good of late."

"Is that so, my friend? And you have a reason, perhaps, for its failure?"

Lao sipped his tea. When he put down his bowl it was to smile politely at the three of them.

"Trade ebbs and flows. It is the tide which comes to cover the mud flats of a man's thin purse. You are visiting other friends of your esteemed grandfather?"

"Those I can find — yes."

"You will be able to discover the honorable Abdul Hakroun still in business."

"That is good hearing."

Kane watched Lorens and the trader narrowly. In that exchange of bland sentences information had been asked for and given. And he intended to be let in on the secret as soon as possible.

But Lorens didn't keep the secret long. "So that's it," he muttered as they came out of Lao's shop. "Abdul Hakroun is abroad — "

"I don't care to appear unduly stupid," cut in Sam, "but just who is Abdul Hakroun?"

The half smile Kane had learned to watch for quirked

Lorens' lips.

"Some men in these latitudes would tell you — quite seriously — that Abdul Hakroun is the Devil. I would hesitate before going so far as to state that. But he does — as you Americans so aptly say — have a finger in every pie up and down the Indies. A very shrewd and clever gentleman. As far as I have ever heard he was only bested once in a bargain. But, of course, any man who would go up against Datu Cooms was asking for failure — "

"Datu Cooms — the former owner of the opal lizard?" inquired Kane.

"The same. He is one of the legends of these parts. According to the most reliable account he was first mate of a Confederate commerce raider starting a cruise in these waters just as your War Between the States came to an end. Cooms chose to remain in this part of the world and drifted to the Sulus. He turned Mohammedan after a time and won the favor of the current sultan, to whom he became a sort of military and naval adviser. The Moros were, as you have doubtles heard, in a constant state of rebellion against their Spanish overlords. Cooms was highly successful and was able to cut out an island kingdom of his own. He lived to be an old man, but to the end of his life he was a fighter few cared to dispute. Abdul Hakroun had a trading war with him once — I believe that there was a pearl fishery in question — and lost.

"Rumor says that Abdul is of the old line of Sulu sultans, and his power hereabouts is unquestioned. Apparently even the Japanese dared not interfere with him. And so now he's busy again, is he? I wonder — "

Abruptly Lorens turned and started back along the wharf at a pace which caught the Americans napping. He headed for the place where the ship's boat which had brought them ashore was still tied up.

"Give," panted Kane as he caught up. "What's the trouble?"

Sword In Sheath   **51**

"If it is as I now think, *it* is trouble! Hakroun or his agents may wish to keep other traders out of the southern waters for a while. The *Sumba* is the first independent trader to sail for the Banda region — "

"You mean that this Hakroun guy may be behind the Guru joke?" asked Sam. "But what would be his object — he can't hope to keep traders out indefinitely. Unless he has a Hitler complex. What reason — "

"I can think of at least four. But van Bleeker must know of this. Do you wish to return to the *Sumba* with me or remain here?"

"Oh, we'll tag along." Kane dropped into the boat. "You have me kind of interested in this Hakroun. I don't like Hitlers — tin pot or otherwise."

They found van Bleeker in his own cabin, a ledger spread open on his desk, a scowl twisting his sunbleached eyebrows.

"Freeing one's self from ghost troubles is a costly business," he greeted them. "If I find our so humorous stowaway he shall speedily wish that he had never arrived to encumber the earth! Shillings and dollars — !" He slammed shut the ledger and settled back in his chair.

"And to what do I owe the pleasure of this visit, gentlemen? Has my bosun run amuck or are there leaks below the waterline? For all calamities I am now ready and prepared."

"Abdul Hakroun is in business again — and flourishing." Lorens doubled one long leg under him in what appeared a most uncomfortable position on the settee.

Van Bleeker did not answer at once. Instead he pulled open a metal-lined box and chose with great care one of the strong black cigars which he delighted in and which his present companions had all refused in turn to try.

"Perhaps" — he clicked the wheel of an old lighter — "I had better at once declare myself bankrupt. Why, tell me truthfully, should I stand a voyage south and work my

weary bones to the grave now? When Hakroun is abroad
it is wise for the honest man to take cover. What devil-
ment is he engaged in at present?"

"I don't know. Lao told me only that he was busy — but
it can't be good — "

Van Bleeker threw up his hands. "When was Hakroun's business ever good — for the other fellow? But it
must be something big — very big — to bring the old man
out these days. He must be near to a hundred years old.
And he retired — when was it? Back in '36 or '37 sometime."

"Retired? His breed never retire. But you are right, he
must have something big in hand, or Lao wouldn't have
hinted it to me."

"You trust Lao?"

"I trust Lao because he just engaged the House to do
some work for him. If it wasn't for that I don't think he
would have spoken — you may depend upon it."

The captain drew deeply on his cigar. "Could it be
Cooms' treasure?"

Lorens laughed. "That will-o'-the-wisp? If Cooms ever
had a treasure it was scattered to the four seas long ago.
In fact, I think we were looking at a good bit of it not an
hour ago. No, I can't picture Hakroun hunting treasure,
even in a senile decline — he has a liking for certainties."

"I don't know," van Bleeker disagreed. "Hakroun lost
that pearling war with the Datu, and he lost face over it —
lost it so badly that half the Indies dared to laugh at him
— for a while. If he could produce Cooms' fabled hoard
now — Well, in a way it would be regaining something he
wants even more than rupees. 'Face' means a lot, more
than we can guess."

But Lorens still shook his head. "No, I don't believe
that it's treasure. But he must have something in line.
Conditions in the south are chaotic. Now is the time for a
smart man to snap up some choice bits here and there."

"Else why would we be sailing there ourselves? Yes, tiger sharks will gather to any kill. And Hakroun is the king shark of them all. If he doesn't fancy visitors — well, that may be just the reason for calling to say 'good day'. And if he was behind this ghost business, it will give me the greatest of pleasure to show him just how muddling are the agents he now employs."

The light in Lorens' eyes equalled the resolve in the captain's stiff jaw. Kane looked to Sam. Imperceptibly the Nisei nodded. This was going to be fun of the sort for which they had both acquired a taste.

"You can count us in — " began Kane.

Van Bleeker gave his sharp bark of laughter. "I pity Hakroun, I honestly do. The world has changed somewhat, and he may discover that Cooms was not the only specimen of his kind in existence. Yes, I find it in me to pity the Hadji Abdul!"

"Where is this Hakroun now?" Kane asked.

"If he is at home, he is in Manado, the northern port of Celebes. He keeps a kind of feudal state there with a dozen sons for bodyguards and an army of retainers. To say nothing of a private navy! Only the Japanese may have disposed of that."

"The *Sumba* sails for Manado, doesn't she?" Lorens inquired innocently.

"That was my intention, yes. Most convenient. You will be able to pay your respects to Hakroun — he was an acquaintance of your grandfather, was he not?"

"Yes. The Jonkheer had a liking for the rogue. If you can get Hakroun to pledge his word he will hold to it — come what disasters there may. Only — "

"Only he does that but once or twice in a lifetime," the captain pointed out. "But in any case you have an excellent reason for making a formal call. And so have these gentlemen. For who knows more of the southern islands than Hakroun with his private intelligence system? So a visit to him would be a logical move for you to make, Mr. Kane. I think that we shall all look forward to Manado. But I wish I knew just what old Abdul now conceals up that very wide sleeve of his!"

"It means money — whatever it is." Lorens turned the wide silver band he wore on his right wrist around and around. "Big money. Oil?"

The captain shook his head. "No. The government would be on to that at once. He wouldn't have a chance to exploit it. My guess is — pearls!"

The silver band was still.

"Pearls!" Lorens' voice was hardly more than a hoarse whisper.

"They have always been Hakroun's first love. You know the stories they tell about his fabulous collection. Suppose — just suppose — he has a clue to a new fishery — one untouched before. Or maybe he has just caught up with Cooms again after all these years. No one ever did find out where the Datu got those five beauties he sold to Hakroun. Yes, pearls it must be."

"I want very much to visit Manado!" Lorens uncurled his legs.

"So do we all, I think. We sail tonight."

5

"HE IS AS A TIGER
AMONG YOUNG GOATS!"

"What in this wide and beautiful world — !"

Kane stopped just within the door of the wardroom and stared at the sparkling bits of light heaped upon a linen square. Lorens' brown fingers were busy there, selecting and rejecting almost as if they had some wizardry of their own to distinguish best from better.

The Netherlander glanced up. "Just a few of my well-gotten gains. Don't believe too much in their value. Were this one an emerald now" — the right forefinger pushed a dark green stone well away from its fellows — "were this an emerald, I might be able to retire to a country villa and spend the rest of my days in idle luxury. Indeed a pleasing prospect. Unfortunately it is only a peridot — good enough but hardly in the emerald class."

"I see. All are not diamonds which glitter." But the fascinating pile of color drew the American to the table as it had earlier pulled Sam. For the Nisei was sitting across from Lorens as intent upon the collection as was its owner.

"At least even I can identify that one." The ex-sergeant indicated a carved drop which might once have been part of an earring. "Precious coral from Japan, isn't it? Mother has a charm like that — we used to play with it when we were kids."

"Yes. Excellent piece too. I think it can be re-set in a clip. Now here we have cat's-eyes, which are coming back into fashion again. And there is a bit of carved amber from Burma. Now this one" — he held a dark stone up to the light — "ought to sell well in China. It's a bloodstone, and the design carved on it is that of a conventionalized bat — such a combination means that it is an amulet which gives its wearer sure power over night demons."

"Hmmm — " Kane touched the gem. "Quite a handy pocket piece, I must say. Any idea of the number and quality of demons accompanying it — are they in good working order? You ought to be able to give some sort of guarantee with it, you know — "

"I am sorry, but I have not yet put it to the test. You may if you wish."

"Fei-ts'ui-yu!" Sam's cry broke through their banter. He was cupping in his palm what seemed to be a bit of frozen green light.

"The kingfisher jade — yes. That is the only piece I have. The best jade rarely leaves China. What we in the West receive is inferior to that. There you have a butterfly amulet, symbol of successful love, considered the proper gift to send to one's beloved. Only you'd have to have rather a deep purse to send that particular butterfly."

"Aren't you worried about the risk of carrying all this around with you?" Kane wanted to know.

"Oh, I keep it locked up in the ship's safe most of the time. I only took it out now to catalogue my most recent purchases — and to do some gloating. You understand — to be successful in gem trading you must love jewels for themselves — more than for the prices they will bring. I am afraid that that is just what I do — "

"Afraid?"

"Yes, afraid. It is because this sort of thing is in my blood — as you Americans say. My earliest memories were of sitting with the Jonkheer while he classified and examined his collection. I knew the feel of a diamond, the look of a sapphire, the beauty of an emerald before I could spell out my own name. And that was how my grandfather had learned the trade before me, and his father before him — back to the first van Norreys who pioneered these waters and set up for an island Raja in the days of the spice trade. And with many of us of the House this interest took the place of more human ties — it did with the Jonkheer. There may come a day when I shall have to choose between such as these and what is a real part of most men's lives — a home and family. When and if that time comes this hunger bred into me may decide my choice. But perhaps that won't be such an evil thing after all. I have learned to follow a lonely path these past few years — "

"Gems before people," Sam mused. "Maybe they won't ever let you down, but me, I'd take people. And so would you, Dutch." He turned to Kane. "We're made that way. But when I look at this stuff, I can see your point — "

"Now we're getting morbid, which is not good at all. And I assure you that a gem buyer in the field has no chance to forget the world. It is only when one retires to an ivory tower to gather one's treasure about one that the danger is present."

"Is there a good market for jewels now? I should think with all the war loot flying about it would be rather risky to do any buying — "

"Not much war loot still flies about — in Europe. Much is being identified and returned to the proper owners — if they are still above ground. For a year I worked upon that very job. We possessed in the records of the House many descriptions of famous jewels which we had bought or sold fifty, a hundred, even two hundred years ago. With those to aid them the Allied Commission was able to trace many pieces."

"Regular detective work!" exclaimed Kane.

"Very much detective work — the kind which when written about in books makes 'thrillers'. I found it most useful to keep me busy — and from thinking too much on other matters. Then I made one very big fool of myself, letting some kind of a bug bite me. And the doctor said, 'No more of this tramping about the continent, young man. Get away, forget the past. Go for six months or a year.' So I came out here to see what I could salvage from the House holdings. Thus I end up on the *Sumba*, and my luck turns from bad to good at last."

"Has it been all bad then?" Kane dared to ask.

Lorens' attention was all for the silver band on his wrist. When he did answer, his voice was both brusque and harsh. "I am not as poorly off as are many of my countrymen. I was caught by the Gestapo — before the liberation. But they had no proof against me — only suspicion. So I did not end against a wall — lucky to do so. Instead I went to a camp. I lived, when others" — he hesitated and turned the band — "did not. Afterwards I had many affairs to settle, and one forgets things — if you can close your mind against memory. That is the best way. Only none of us are the same persons we were five years ago — we never shall be again. Tell me — is that good luck or bad?"

"Luck is what you make it," countered Sam.

"*Fortunam facio*, eh? Others must have reached that same conclusion long ago. 'I make my luck' was engraved on a sword hilt I saw once, a sword hilt out of Rome. Well, I have not yet had to invert Ganesha to bring him to terms — that is true."

"Invert Ganesha?" asked Sam.

"I know that one," Kane chuckled. "You turn the Indian god of luck upside down to make him treat you properly. You once did that in Sumatra, didn't you, Lorens?"

"No, I discovered him in that undignified position, left so by some angry householder, and turned him right again. That should have brought us his smiles afterward. Perhaps it did — we escaped successfully."

"Pardon, mijnheer." The steward came soft-footed to the table. "Capt. van Bleeker says Manado is now sighted — "

"Thank you, Akim. Here, if you wish to make your-selves useful" — Lorens pushed toward the Americans rolls of flannel in which innumerable small pockets had been sewn — "help me pack these — one piece to a pocket."

Once his teasure had been locked away all three climbed to the bridge of the *Sumba*. Celebes lay before them, her broken backbone of mountains blue and misty across the sky, her ragged coastline still only a black smudge against the sea. On the map the great island sprawled like an octopus with arms flung questingly to three points of the compass. But what Kane saw now was not on a map. It was so much larger than he had pictured it —

Manado lay at the far tip of the longest arm — the one which pointed from west to east out into the Molucca Strait. Perhaps a mile out from the breakwater which sheltered the town was the island volcano of Manado Tua, and, back of the widely sprawled city itself, was Klabat, a second threatening mountain whose flaming heart was not yet dead.

The *Sumba* wore in and anchored before a trading post as old as the spice trade itself, though nowadays the principal cargo to be found on the water-rotted wharves was not the 'black rose' of the clove or the aromatic cinnamon but awkward bundles of rattan.

"Well, gentlemen." Capt. van Bleeker came back from his polite meeting with port authorities. "What are your plans for today?"

Kane settled his sunhelmet more firmly. "We're playing the inquiring tourist on shore. Any suggestions, captain?"

"None — unless it is to visit the Hadji Abdul Hakroun."

"He *is* here then?" A light frown deepened a line between Sam's widely spaced brows, a sign that the ex-sergeant was engaged in serious thinking.

"Oh, yes, he is here. See that tidy little coaster across the harbor there? She is the *Drinker of the Wind* — and closer to the old man than the blood in his veins. When she is in port, then you will find His Excellency in residence."

"That being so," observed Lorens, "I must preserve my reputation for good manners. A duty call upon the person of my grandfather's old acquaintance is clearly indicated — especially when I am traveling for the sole purpose of re-establishing old ties."

"You won't care if we tag along on this dutiful mission?" asked Kane.

"Not at all. After all, your business would lead you there sooner or later anyway. Hakroun knows more about your islands than any other living man. But I suggest that we dress more formally. The Hadji affects a state which nowadays even minor royalty would find difficult to maintain. It is well to match his standards when possible."

So in white suits, tormented by the collars of civilization fastened to the last button, they went ashore some time later.

Manado was a wide-flung town of native thatched huts set far apart. There was a European quarter, of course, consisting of the hotel and the Harmonie Club, built and garnished by homesick Netherlands exiles, and one of western style houses. But Lorens skirted these evidences of their own civilization and led them along a way which was more dirt lane than city street until they came to a white wall. Following this they found a pair of gates — broad enough to admit a marching regiment — barred with greenish metal.

As they hesitated, a small postern in the larger barrier swung open, and a pure-blood Malay, a man of some position judging by his silk turban, stood watching them. When Lorens inquired in the native tongue for the master of the villa, the guard stood aside and motioned them into a courtyard where Malays, Sea-Dykes, and a Moro or two lounged at ease. None of these raised their eyes or gave any sign that they saw the three.

Sam moved up beside Kane until their shoulders were almost brushing; his dark eyes flashed from one of those elaborately blank-faced guards to another. There was something of the spider's parlor about this stronghold of a Moro trader.

The Malay doorkeeper pulled aside a leather curtain, the smooth surface of which was stamped with colored designs. He did not enter with them or even announce their coming, only waved them through to an inner court.

This was a much smaller one and rugs of silken luxuriance were heaped to serve as seats of a kind. On three such mats were three men. Two arose as Lorens and the Americans entered, but the third only looked up.

Live eyes shone from a face which might have been pictured in wild fantasy. In the first place — to say that the man was old was an understatement. The head beneath the band of the emerald green turban was that of a patriarch who might have witnessed the march of the great Alexander. For it was no face — it was a skull with ivory velum stretched paper-thin over handsome bones. A point of white beard masked chin and jaw, but the proudly hooked nose was a bird's beak — a hawk's beak. Brows sprouted thickly above the shrunken caverns which sheltered those eyes of fire — young and vigorous fire. Abdul Hakroun was an old, old man, but those eyes testified that he had lost none of his interest in the world.

"May the Peace of Allah, the Compassionate, the Ever-Understanding, be upon you, son of my friend's son. Welcome to the House of Hakroun — "

The voice which issued from between those dried and sunken lips was even more startling than the alive eyes. It was not the shrill cackle of extreme age, but a rich, lilting chant.

Lorens bowed and Kane found himself imitating that gesture clumsily. There was something about the Hadji Abdul which pulled such courtesies out of a man. The Netherlander murmured the proper greeting, then introduced the two Americans.

"Americans, eh" The bright eyes searched them from scuffed shoes to sweat-dampened hair. "We have had many visits from your countrymen these past few years — but they kept to the air and did not venture closer. Now excuse an old man his thickened wits — this is a most propitious day. Sit, sit, my friends. These are my sons, Mohamet and Kuran. Since I do not sail the seas today they have taken the management of the House interests into their hands — "

Kane watched those eyes instead of the gesturing hands or the bearded mouth. "I bet they have!" He returned mentally to that statement — for he noted that both men, although they were well into middle-age, stood at respectful attention until their father motioned them back to their rug seats.

"And your esteemed grandfather, Tuan van Norreys, how is it with him?"

"The Jonkheer has been dead these five years, sir. He died on the day of the Nazi occupation of my country — "

A brown claw plucked gently at the silver beard. "Ah, so. Well, for Azrael's visits there is no remedy. Do not the Chinese say most truly — 'Death is a black camel which kneels unbidden at every compound gate'? But for you, my son, I grieve. His loss is one not to be reckoned, save within the heart. Ah, here is refreshment. Drink deep, I beg of you, the day is hot and your path has been a dusty one — "

Kuran took the tray from the servant's hands and presented it himself to the guests. Kane tasted the pinkish liquid in the tall rock crystal goblet and found it to be a sweetish syrup, agreeably cool.

"Is it in your mind, Tuan van Norreys, to reopen once more the Jonkheer's trade?" Abdul's fingers still played with his beard.

"As far as it lies within my power to do so I shall follow where he led, yes."

"And you, my friends." Hakroun addressed Kane. "You, too, are dealers in gems?"

The American shook his head. "No. We are hunting for a lost countryman of ours. He was the pilot on one of the bombers sent to raid this island. He and his plane never returned. There may be a chance that some survivor is still alive on an uncharted island — "

Now the brown fingers were still for a second before they were hidden again in the soft curls of hair.

"An adventurous quest surely, and one which will occupy you for long. In these seas are many, many islands — some not on any map."

"That is why we asked Mr. van Norreys to bring us to you," Kane returned boldly. "We heard that you have, sir, many business contacts in the islands and we had hopes that you might be able to aid us with some clue — "

Abdul was giving the younger man his full attention now. But when Kane finished Hakroun was only sorrowful to give disappointment.

"It is true that the House of Hakroun has many contacts and sources of information through the southern seas. Only this dawn did one of my grandsons return from a protracted voyage to Amboina. But among the many tales he heard there were none concerning an American castaway. Land which may not be marked on your western-made maps is fully known to the Sea-Dykes and to my men also. And nowhere is there an unacccounted-for American. I fear your quest to be a fruitless one. Lost airplanes have plunged into the sea many times and, in their passing, left no mark upon the waters. I would that I could help you in this search, but I believe that no man living has the information that will aid you."

"Thank you, sir, for your advice." Kane was polite enough.

"You expect to follow it?" Were those eyes laughing at him?

"We cannot abandon our search so soon. There is always hope — "

"Always hope, yes. How could we mortals live if it were not for hope — which is also sometimes a deadly demon leading men to full destruction."

Kane put down his goblet. Was that a hint of threat? But Abdul had lost interest in him. The old Moro was turning now to Lorens, and something in the set of the Netherlander's shoulders argued that van Norreys had been waiting for just that.

"You have had a successful trip so far?" was Hakroun's opening move.

"As good as can be hoped for in the unsettled state of

the islands. The Japanese swept the strongboxes bare where they could. I sail now to attempt to re-fasten old ties."

"And did you tighten such a one when you visited the honorable Lao in Jolo?"

"He had some black coral — of fine quality. It is a novelty which may catch the favor of the American market where it is not yet widely known."

"Black coral. But do you not find coral less of interest than say — rubies?" prodded Abdul.

"I am a designer as well as a merchant. Much can be done with stones of lesser value. But have you rubies to sell, sir?"

Abdul appeared lost in thought for a moment, then he clicked his fingers at Kuran. From somewhere within his loose robes the man produced a lacquer box which he handed to his father. Hakroun twisted off the top and dipped out a long chain which supported a gem-set medallion. He handed it over to Lorens and settled back to await the Netherlander's reaction.

"Where did this come from?" Van Norreys' voice was colorless and even.

"In times of war many treasures come to light from old hiding places. This was given to me for sale. Would the House of Norreys be interested? The stones are good — "

"They are of oriental cut and would have to be re-cut for our western market. Also the Mani Mala and the Nararatna have no value abroad. Perhaps in India you could drive a good bargain." Lorens handed back the flashing chain.

Whether this firm refusal of his offering displeased Abdul or not, Kane could not guess. But within a very short time they were ushered out, suavely enough. When they stood in the road again Lorens kicked at a stone viciously.

Sword In Sheath

"The old devil!" he snorted. "Trying to catch me like that! Did he think that I was so green in the trade? But I'd give quite a lot from a none too full purse to know where he lifted that — fourteenth-century work, every bit of it!"

"You mean that you think that necklace thing was stolen?" demanded Kane.

"I don't see how he could have gotten it any other way. Those things are guarded better than some kings' lives — they mean the good or bad fortune of a whole house or dynasty. And suppose I had bought it, or even accepted it to sell on commission, and the real owner appeared. Phew!" He snapped thumb and finger together. "That would be the end of Norreys right there."

Sam looked back at the wall of Abdul Hakroun's stronghold and spat out a sentence in a dialect which Kane had never heard. But Lorens answered with a curt laugh.

"That is to the point! 'He is a tiger among young goats.' Only today I do not wear either horns or hooves, no matter how brightly Hadji Abdul's stripes gleam!"

6

"HE WAS FROM
THE FORBIDDEN LAND, TUAN!"

With the uneasy feeling that the old Moro trader had had the best of their encounter, the three from the *Sumba* trudged back toward the European quarter of Manado. Lorens suggested that it might be well to look up van Bleeker at the Harmonie Club, but Kane disagreed.

"Sam and I are only tourists. We'll have a reason for poking around in the native town. Hakroun can't be the only pebble on this beach. Maybe we can contact one of those famous turtle hunters who are supposed to know so much about out-of-the-way islands. I'd like to ask some leading questions — and some about the pious Hadji too!"

"That is my mission also. But I shall do the asking among my own countrymen. We may meet later at the club if you wish." Lorens turned aside, and the Americans strolled on alone.

"Cigaretten?"

The thin pipe came from somewhere about their knees. Kane mechanically felt for the pack in his pocket, and a very small and very thin native boy watched that gesture with hungry and hopeful eyes.

"Cigarettes, is it? Okay." Kane flipped a couple from the package into the dirty little paw.

Both the boy and his loot vanished as Sam shook his head reprovingly. "Will you never learn, Dutch? In about a half a second that kid'll be back with most of the town mooching for handouts, and they'll hound us the rest of the afternoon. Cigarettes are treasures they're not going to allow to escape them."

Fearing just such a development they quickened their pace and slid into a narrow lane between two nipa-thatched huts. Kane almost jostled a man hesitating there in the shadow, a man who dared to touch Sam's coat sleeve, a singularly bold move for a native.

Only this was no Malay, Moro, or ex-head-hunting Toradja from the interior. At his first hissed word Sam stopped short to face a Japanese.

"This is a small trader — on his beam ends," Marusaki translated rapidly for Kane. "Wants to get out of here if he can manage to raise the price of a passage. He wants to show us what he has left for sale — "

"What about it? Story ring true to you?"

Sam eyed the cringing man. "Maybe eighty percent of it's okay. He's scared, clean through. I'd trust him as far as I could keep an eye on him. Says he just got in from the south and wants to get out of here — but quick. He's got the right idea at that — these islands are no place for his sort now — not if they want to keep their heads and their skins."

"Let's see what he's got to offer then."

The Japanese ducked into the least attractive of the two huts as if he had little liking for the open air of

Manado. Once inside he made a great show of hospitality, tugging out two boxes to serve as seats, then opening up a wicker hamper.

What he had to see was mostly worthless trash, odds and ends of island goods, tawdry and useless. But Sam made a sudden swoop into a muddle of small bits and came up with a large silver coin. He went to the doorway of the hut to inspect his find in the light.

"Hey, what year was it that our American tea clippers first blew into these islands, Dutch?"

"I don't know — back in the 1820s or '30s, I think. Why?"

"Looks like I'm holding a little memento of those days. U.S. silver dollar — date 1840. Wonder where our friend picked this up?" The Nisei loosed a flood of Japanese on the trader while Kane took the coin.

Sam was right, it was a silver dollar from their own country, and fairly unworn too. How long had it been knocking around the islands? Ever since some Yankee skipper had parted with it perhaps a hundred years before?

"Where'd he say he got it?"

"He doesn't know. Was passed to him in trade somewhere south. He may be lying." Sam shrugged. "It'd make a good lucky piece. I'm buying it."

"Did you ask him about the southern islands?"

"That's a thought!" Again Sam launched into the hissing crackle of his ancestors' native tongue, and his questions loosed a floodgate in reply. Kane caught the name 'Hakroun' repeated several times and never with either reverence or liking. Sam listened intently, interrupting now and again with other questions which acted upon the trader as might goads upon a maddened bull. But when the man seemed to be actually talked out, Sam took his wallet and counted out several bills. So in the end they left the little man bowing and hissing as if he had been wound up by clockwork to perform only those two functions.

"What did he have to say?"

"Plenty. This Hakroun gent is practically running the trading hereabouts. Our friend back there did fairly well as long as the Japs were in power. But when they pulled out the old Moro took over — but good. The Hadji's frozen out most of the small traders now and has everything pretty much his own way. For one thing, he doesn't encourage any exploring expeditions to nose around south of Besi in the Soelas — "

"Now I wonder why?"

"So do a lot of other people apparently. The consensus of opinion at present is that the old gentleman is onto something pretty big and intends to keep it in his own pocket."

"Any suggestion as to what that something big might be?"

"Oh, there are several different ones, ranging from buried treasure to oil. But everyone is certain it is a rich find. Hakroun doesn't trouble to deal in anything less than millions. Anyway, he and his agents discourage southern travel. Where does that leave us?"

"If I know van Bleeker it leaves us preparing for a fight. I don't think the captain is going to honor any 'No Trespassing' signs if they interfere with his own plans — he's as much as said that already. But what about our own little problem of the missing man? That trader have any bright ideas on the subject?"

"He said that hundreds could be hiding out down there, there's room enough — "

"Hiding out voluntarily, yes. But marooned involuntarily, I wonder. Hiding out — Does that expression give you any ideas now? Did he use just that term?"

"He did!"

Kane grinned. "Ironjaw might be amused at that. 'Hiding out', a very thought-provoking term. We had better do a little poking around down south too."

"Haven't you always intended to?"

"Naturally. And now we have such a good excuse for being stubborn about it too!"

Beaming contentedly upon the world, as represented by the dust, smells and heat of Manado, they turned back toward the Harmonie Club and the company of Lorens, whom they discovered seated by himself at a table in the bar.

"Where's all the population?" Kane surveyed the somewhat bare room.

"Most of them are not back from captivity yet, I gather." The Netherlander shut the notebook in which he had been scribbling. "The plantations have not begun to produce again, and the *Sumba* is one of the first privately owned vessels to touch this port since the war ended. Did you get a good look at the town?"

"We did some shopping. Show him your new luck piece, Sam."

The Nisei rang the dollar on the table, and Lorens picked it up.

"We think it's a remainder from the clipper ship days — when the tea trade was on with China — lots of our ships in these waters then," Kane explained.

But the Netherlander had taken out a jeweler's glass and was now examining one side of the coin closely.

"What is it? Secret writing or something?" asked Sam.

To their surprise Lorens was sober enough when he answered. "Almost that. In the first place this has been someone else's lucky piece. See this tiny hole — that was made for a ring — perhaps to suspend the coin from a watch chain. And there *is* something scratched on it — "

"What?"

"The letters 'R' and 'S' and the numerals '1944'."

"R and S — Rodney Safield!"

"Or maybe Rudolph Schmidt," returned Sam to his companion's jubilation. "More than one man in this world has those two initials. Did his father say anything about his having such a luck charm?"

Kane tried to remember the details on that sheet of identification particulars they had received from Col. Thurston. But he was sure there had been no mention of such a coin.

"Coincidence is a strange thing," commented Lorens. "You may not be right about this dollar — and then again it may be a real clue. Where did you get it?"

But Sam was already on his feet. "Clue or not, I'm going back and have another talk with that trader. If he thinks we mean business about this he may open up — "

With Kane and Lorens at his heels, the ex-sergeant wove back through the hut maze to the shelter which had been a squatting place for the Japanese merchant. But now no one came in answer to Sam's hail, and when the three crowded into the dusky room it was to find it empty of both occupant and trade goods.

"Hi!" Kane jumped through the door and clamped hands on a small naked figure who wriggled as desperately as a fish for an instant, then hung limp and shivering in the American's grip. "He was peeking around the corner at us," explained the captor. "Where has the trader gone?" he asked his captive in Coast-Malay.

Yellow-white half moons showed in the corners of wide frightened eyes as the small boy kept his attention on Kane's face. But he remained steadfastly dumb to all the urging of both Americans and even to the less excited coaxing of the Netherlander.

"Please — you wish to know something? I might help — "

Braced by one hand against the wall of the deserted hut stood a straight-backed native. He wore drill

Sword In Sheath

trousers as white and spotless as their own, but the side arch of his brown chest and the breadth of his shoulders were bare. There was no turban covering his ´close-clipped black hair, and he spoke in English, clearly but slowly, as if dragging the necessary words from the depths of memory.

"There was a trader here a little while ago," Kane began. He was trying to guess which island claimed this man for its own. The fellow was neither Arab nor Chinese, and with that height and build he was unlike any Filipino the American had seen so far. On the other hand he did not resemble a Moro or Solomon Islander. His wide, pleasantly smiling mouth with its unfiled white teeth was not stained the scarlet of a betel chewer, and his standard of personal cleanliness was manifestly high.

"A trader — here?" The stranger managed to suggest polite incredulity in an inoffensive fashion. "But this hut has been deserted for weeks. It has a bad name among the townspeople — they say that it has housed a demon."

The small boy still in Kane's grasp spat out a frenzied string of words, then tore free from the American's relaxed hold, diving between the two huts and so out of reach. His screech left the tall native frowning.

"What did he say just then?" Kane wanted to know.

"That the demon returned but has gone again. So there has been someone here." He slid into the hut, and Kane saw him making a thorough search of the one musty room.

"What was this trader, please? Moro, Arab, Chinese?" he asked as he came out with empty hands.

"He was Japanese and in a big hurry to get home," Sam returned shortly.

Again those white teeth showed in a quick flash of smile. "If he was Japanese, it is easy to believe that he wished to return home. The islanders do not greatly love their late masters. But this man is necessary to you now — yes?"

"Suppose you tell us first why you are so interested in our affairs." Sam faced the taller man, his hands resting lightly on his hips, not too far from the weapon he had strapped on that morning as a matter of course.

"But certainly I will tell you. Because, sirs, I have been following you in the hope that I might be of service. I am Jasper Fortnight from American Samoa."

"American Samoa — that's half the ocean away!" broke in Kane.

"Yes, it is indeed far from here. But in wartime many men travel to far places. I was mate of a trading schooner which was sunk by the Japanese in these waters. Now I wait for a ship to take me away again. I hold a mate's ticket, you understand.

"Meanwhile, here in Celebes I am clerk to Kasteen Lowe at the hotel. Your ship, the *Sumba*, is the first to touch this port in weeks. It is my hope to find a berth aboard her. So I followed you. I speak many island dialects, and I hoped that you might recommend me to the *Sumba*'s captain. You will?"

"Suppose first you do us this service," suggested Lorens. "Discover more about the present whereabouts of this Japanese trader."

"Let me speak with his neighbors." Fortnight started briskly toward the nearest occupied hut. "Many eyes mark all happenings in Manado, and all that passes here is known to at least a few." He called a sentence or two through the hut doorway and after a long moment of silence was answered. But the speaker did not edge out into their sight, and it was plain that the occupants of the hut were none too well pleased to be so singled out.

Kane nudged Sam. "What dialect is he speaking?"

"I don't know — probably some local one. Quite helpful, isn't he? Just brimming over with good will and Boy Scoutishness — "

Jasper came back in two strides. "Your trader has been here for two days. But no man bought from him or sold to him, and none saw him go — "

"Actual or willful blindness?" asked Kane.

"That I do not know. Perhaps both. If so they will never admit it — "

But he was interrupted by a murmur from the hut, and after listening intently, he threw out his hands in a little gesture of defeat.

"They say that that is all, that they know nothing of this man and to ask more is to arouse the wrath of the demon. They wish us to go away."

"Well" — Lorens pushed up his helmet — "that is all. I can vouch for that. Not even torture would gain you more. Shall we go farther afield?"

"Sure! He may have vanished in a puff of dust here but I don't believe that he'll head inland — not with the natives against him. The Toradjas were head-hunters once, and some of them may still have a hankering to try that ancestral sport. The authorities wouldn't ask too many questions about a missing Jap. But if he went to sea surely someone down at the harbor saw him go."

They started on, and Fortnight followed. Apparently he was not going to allow his chance for a berth on the *Sumba* to escape him. Kane glanced back at him once or twice, measuringly. The Samoan was friendly, and there was something likeable in that easy smile and unruffled poise. Whether he was a resourceful and energetic job hunter or a very smooth and accomplished liar was yet to be proved. Hakroun had this town in his pocket by all accounts, and this man might well be one of the old Moro's smarter operators.

Faced by the bustling activity of the harbor where the small native vessels were loading and discharging cargo, Sam hesitated, and Kane asked innocently, "Where do we begin now? If the fellow wants to hide — it'd take a regular shore patrol to route him out here. And if everyone clams up about seeing him — where does that leave us?"

Sam scowled and plowed through the shore refuse toward a group of natives who were holding a conference above tide level. One of them turned to spit out a mouthful of scarlet betel juice and caught sight of the Nisei. He did not even hurry; it was as if he valued Sam too low to pay the American the respect of a hasty retreat. Instead he was almost lazy about rising to his feet and languid in his drift down shore, a drift in which his companions joined.

"See that?" Marusaki demanded. "This demon trader business must be hot — plenty hot — "

"So one would begin to suspect," Lorens agreed. "Or else it may just be that Hakroun has ceased to smile upon us and said so — publicly. Fortnight, can you ask questions without receiving the response accorded a leper?"

"I can try, sir, if you wish."

Sam pulled at his lower lip and scowled sullenly but Kane nodded. So Fortnight left them and struck back towards the town. As he went his shoulders sagged, and he kept his eyes on the deep dust of the roadway. He was the picture of a man who had been refused a job. Kane watched the Samoan out of sight. Enemy or friend, Fortnight was good — but definitely good! Now he would probably go around telling about how he'd been turned down and tongues might loosen. Yeah, Fortnight knew all the tricks. But who *was* Fortnight?

"Good, isn't he?" he asked Sam.

"Too blamed good! You can't tell me he isn't an old hand at the game — "

"To that fact I agree." Lorens reached out for the cigarette Kane proffered, but his hand was not quite steady. When the Netherlander became aware of that tremor the hollows below his cheek bones flushed, and he gripped the tube so that the tobacco sifted from torn paper.

"Old terrors die hard," he commented with a little embarrassed laugh. "After the last few years I find I do not care for events or persons I cannot satisfactorily explain. Even the sound of shoe leather on stone — when he who wears it is a heavy walker — is apt to be upsetting — especially at night. You must excuse such folly — "

"We have a few pet memories ourselves," Kane interrupted. "Now I find sharpened bamboo canes very unattractive, and Sam has no great affection for large mottled branches in jungle trees — they might become live members of the reptile clan. But Fortnight — "

"Cigaretten, Tuan?"

"Hello! You back?" The small beggar was there again, this time both dirty hands outstretched and a confident smile creasing his sticky face.

"Cigaretten?" He voiced his plea for the second time. And when Kane did not display the open-handedness of their first encounter, he added in a low voice, "Hij is — " He stopped tantalizingly, watching the cigarettes.

"He is — Who is?" Kane dropped one cigarette into the dirty hand and drew another from the package.

"The trader — he is gone — "

A second cigarette joined the first.

"Back to his demon place, Mijnheer Amerikaan. He was from the Forbidden Land — "

"The Forbidden Land — but what — ?"

But the boy was quick. He grabbed the pack of cigarettes from Kane's fingers and was away, dodging with expert ease Sam's grab.

"The Forbidden Place." Both Americans turned to Lorens for enlightenment.

"Might be anything — or nothing. The natives have given this trader a supernatural origin, that may be all. We can ask van Bleeker."

"Something accomplished, something done." Sam flipped the silver dollar. "Can we, I wonder, make that satisfying statement about this day's work?"

"We can try." Kane jammed his hands into cigarette-empty pockets.

7

"ONE WITH LEMURIA AND ATLANTIS"

"The Forbidden Place, is it?" Van Bleeker smiled a bit loftily. "Man, that is one of the oldest of island legends. I am surprised that you, van Norreys, were taken in by it — you know something of the Indies."

"Does any man know the Indies?" countered Lorens. "As for the Forbidden Place — that story I do not know."

"It is one with Lemuria and Atlantis, a fabled island where a sultan or raja ruled in great peace and plenty, his people knowing neither harm nor want. In fact the men of the Forbidden Place were so satisfied with their lot that they were rumored to have the nasty habit of killing all outsiders who dared to invade their territory, since they had no wish for the sins of the world to enter their paradise."

"Beneath some folk tales there is a core of hard fact," remarked Sam. "What about the base of this one?"

"It is true that there were island kingdoms in the Indies before the coming of European explorers — look at the histories of the Princes of Bali and Java. Waves of immigration from India flowed into these seas. And it might well be true that some half-savage northern raja set himself up in a pocket kingdom hereabouts — although we have found no remains of his glory. The jungle is a great swallower of the romantic past. This raja may even have protected his sovereignty for a generation by murder of all travelers. But at the best he must have flourished some five hundred years ago. So I don't believe your trader had dealings with him — "

"Then you think that there's nothing in the story?"

"No," van Bleeker answered Kane frankly. "But someone may have revived the tale to serve his own ends. I will admit that if Hakroun is busy in this matter there will be trouble."

"We could discover nothing except that several praus have put to sea — the trader could have sailed on one of them."

"It is my opinion, van Norreys, that your trader has vanished from the sight of men permanently. If, for any reason, he had the ill will of Hakroun, he undoubtedly disappeared. I don't like this affair — not one little bit do I like it!"

"Hakroun means trouble, eh?" Kane bit at a ragged quicknail on his thumb. Sam lounged at ease, smoothing the jacket he had just discarded. But Lorens hunched forward, turning the silver band around and around on his bony wrist.

"Hakroun always means trouble!" snapped the captain. "But if he goes against us he will not have a friendless Jap trader to deal with! If Hakroun has re-established the kingdom of the Forbidden Place for his own use he may have invaders."

"What do you suspect he's trying to hide?" Sam wanted to know.

"Something big, and yet something which can be

handled quickly, because he knows that now the war is over the trading companies and government control will be back. He can only play this game for a limited time — therefore his find is something from which he can skim the cream in a hurry. It is not a mine or oil — "

"Which leaves what — "

"Pearls." Lorens dropped the single word into the discussion.

Van Bleeker's breath made a hissing sound through his half-bared teeth. There was a visible hunger in his weathered face. "Pearls!" he repeated, and his fingers crooked upon the table top as if reaching for the gleaming globes of frozen sea light. "Yes, that would certainly be it — pearls! A new fishery — untouched before maybe!"

"But could he work it secretly?" protested Kane. "He'd have to have divers and equipment and — "

"He has the divers. Before the war he had shares in several pearling ships on the Australian Banks. And native divers need no more equipment than goggles, a good knife and a stone for weight. Yes, he could work it easily for a while. Of course, once the government patrol boats begin making their rounds again, his monopoly would be gone. But before that he could take out enough to make a fortune — another one — to hide away in his treasure chests. If the bed has never been fished before and is especially rich, he may make ten fortunes. Pearls are high now — the market has been starved through the war."

"Yes, what is it?" the captain added impatiently a moment later as the steward looked in upon them.

"There is one who comes from the shore. He says that he has a message for the young American lords and that it is an important one."

"Fortnight, I'll bet! He's the Samoan we told you of, sir," Kane explained. "All right to have him in here?"

"Certainly. Bring him here."

It *was* Fortnight who came in. He now wore a shirt and carried a coat over his arm. In his hand was the peaked cap of a ship's officer, although it was marked with no insignia or braid. He greeted van Bleeker with a gesture which was close to a salute before he turned to the Americans.

"Well, what were you able to find out?"

"Much, sir," he answered Kane. "This trader you seek was in Manado several days, but no man knows from whence he came — save that a ship of the Orang-laut, the sea gypsies, put in just at nightfall one day and sailed with the dawn on the next. While he was here no one traded with him, but he had one visitor who came late at night to his hut. There was a quarrel between the two. And after the visitor departed the trader was seen to crawl from his hut and bathe his face in water from the storage place of his neighbor."

"And this visitor?"

"Was undoubtedly identified by the witness who told me this, sir. But his fear was greater than his greed — no offer of mine would bring the truth out of him. However in his struggle not to speak, he forgot to guard against telling other matters. He believed that something was taken from the trader by force, and that the man lingered on here after that in hopes of recovering it."

"The Nararatna!"

"You mean that necklace Hakroun showed you?" Kane asked Lorens.

The Netherlander nodded vigorously. "And I refused to buy," he returned with a glance at the listening Samoan. "It might well be that. In certain quarters it would be worth thousands. It might also be used in blackmail. But if it was the Nararatna which was taken from him — where did he get it in the first place?"

"Let us not stray from the main course now," van

Bleeker cut in. "So this trader lingered on, hoping to regain his property?"

"That is what the witness believed, sir. But after the Americans visited him this afternoon he disappeared. And of that disappearance I could learn nothing at all. It was as if all mention of his going was forbidden."

"Could be at that," Sam observed. "They have a way of clamming up on occasion over things which they believe are none of an outsider's affair. Any other bits of news?"

"Only that in the past hour three men have been summoned to the house of Abdul Hakroun, and one of the three was the captain of the *Drinker of the Wind*."

"Looks as if we've stirred up the anthill. We talk to a trader, and he promptly disappears. We go to visit an old gentleman, and as soon as we leave he sends for his ship's captain. If I were a suspicious man now — " Kane laughed.

But van Bleeker's attention was all for Fortnight. "They tell me that you have a mate's papers — "

From the breast pocket of the coat he was carrying the Samoan pulled a stout envelope from which he shook several folded papers. At the reading of the third one van Bleeker's eyebrows arose, and he laid it down, to study the tall man carefully.

"So you were one of Redfern's men?"

"I was, sir. He taught me all I know."

"What became of Capt. Redfern?"

The Samoan's face did not change expression, but Kane saw his hands twist the edge of his coat.

"We were cruising north in the *Leopard*. Capt. Redfern had not used the radio for several days — he had had a touch of fever. There was a Japanese submarine in those waters, and she blew the bottom out of us before we even knew that war had been declared. That was on December 10, 1941. We took to the boats — or rather to the boat — there was only time to launch one before the *Leopard* went under. The Japanese machine-gunned us, and the captain — the captain was killed, sir. It was two weeks before we survivors were picked up by an American destroyer.

"Since then I have been on cargo ships wherever I could find a berth. Only I am a Samoan, and not all captains were like Michael Redfern — they do not trust a native as an officer — "

"I have my full complement of officers," van Bleeker pointed out.

"I know that, sir. Only I have been here in Manado for some time, and I want to ship out. I was an able seaman before I was Capt. Redfern's mate."

"Very well. Tell Felder to sign you on. I can use a man with your knowledge of the islands."

"Thank you, sir." There was gratitude coloring his voice, but he lost none of his dignity. And he gave van Bleeker an officer's salute as he left the cabin.

"That may be one good thing we found in this port," observed the captain of the *Sumba*.

"How — ?" asked Kane.

"I have heard of Redfern and his methods. If this man is one of Redfern's boys — and his papers state that he is — he is worth two of most modern crews. Michael Redfern was one of the old hands in the island trade. They say that his father sailed out here in the days of the tea trade and never went home again. All the Redferns had the Indies in their blood; they weren't happy away from the coral seas. And Michael Redfern had a strong belief in the natives. In the days when most of the white men treated them like animals, and none too intelligent animals at that, Redfern had the habit of picking up island boys he liked the looks of and giving them educations — training them usually as seamen. He had very few failures, and some of the graduates of his school went on to conquer new worlds. I know of at least two who did very well for themselves. One was in Hawaii before the war, running a sort of tourist bureau, booking cruises through islands off the main line of steamship travel. The other captained his own ship and owned two others in the copra trade. So the Japs got Redfern, did they? Well, there's always a berth on the *Sumba* for one of his boys."

Overhead an orange-lemon moon held steady, and below streaks of cold fire stripped back from the *Sumba*'s bow where the phosphorescence made fantastic patterns on the waves. Kane leaned both elbows on the rail and watched the curl of light lace out. All this talk of Hakroun — Granted that the man was a menace and a tricky one. But there was no doubt that van Bleeker had a few tricks up his jacket sleeve also. Then there was that dollar — R.S., 1944. And in 1944 Rodney Safield had disappeared over this same sea through which they were now cutting their way south.

Van Bleeker's Dutch temper had flared. There had been no trade in Manado — at least none for the master of the *Sumba*. So now they sailed for Besi in the Soelas to try their luck again. And from Besi only a prophet coud foresee where van Bleeker's stubbornness might take them.

"Hiding places" to the south — that Jap trader might have boiled over with a few more facts if they could have cornered him. Maybe Hakroun had something beside a new pearl fishery on his mind. Though Lorens still argued that that was enough to arouse the old shark into trying to keep intruders out of the southern waters. Who could be hiding out? Nazi sub crews? Hold out Japs? Native agitators waiting to descend on Java? There were a lot of fascinating possibilites —

"As Grant took Richmond!"

Kane's hands were suddenly vice-tight about the edge of the rail. There was a sweet taste behind his teeth, along his neck the fine hairs prickled. But he did not turn to face the shadows from which that whisper had come. Instead he answered, steadily enough, "Lincoln freed the slaves."

A good bit more than a year had passed since he had repeated those same words to identify himself to a jungle fighter who had been a collection of badly articulated bones sketchily covered with rags.

"Who are you?" he demanded of the night.

"A friend, Lt. Kane. I had my orders from Capt. Boone to contact you at the first opportunity. We decided that that old password would be my best introduction — "

"Fortnight!" He was able to place that soft murmur now.

"Yes, sir. I have been in the United States' service for some years — after all, I, too, was born on American soil. This is the first time I have been able to approach you when you were alone, lieutenant — "

"You can drop the lieutenant stuff — I'm strictly unoffical now, Fortnight. So you're the contact Boone promised. We might have guessed. Do you have any messages for me?"

"I was about to ask you the same question, sir. There have been many rumors but no real news. Sailing on the *Sumba* was a very lucky thing for all of us — there have been no other ships southward bound for weeks. I have been trying to find one for two months and could not get space even in an outrigger — "

Kane's eyes narrowed as he stared into the night. "That sounds as if someone doesn't want any visitors. Is it Hakroun?"

"I think so — yes. But why I cannot discover. He had no love for the Japanese, even though they did not trouble him while they held the Celebes. It is my thought that they were a little afraid of him. He has more power in these seas than your race understands, sir. Not only is he the true descendant of the last great Moro sultan, but his wealth is unreckoned. What he wishes is law to many men. Yet I believe that Hakroun himself is uneasy now. During the past six weeks he has called in a hundred fighting men and is keeping them at his headquarters. The *Drinker of the Wind* has been armed and cases which could only contain ammunition were transferred to her one night last week."

"Sounds as if he were planning a private war. And you think that's our concern?"

"So much so, that when I reported the facts to Capt. Boone he ordered me to make contact with you, joining forces on the *Sumba*. Capt. van Bleeker must be persuaded to hunt out Hakroun's secret — it is of utmost importance. Capt. Boone believes that it may be the focus point of all the undefinable trouble in the Banda Sea."

"Van Bleeker won't need any of our urging. He's already angry enough to go after Hakroun. He thinks that the old man is spoiling his chances for trade. There's the affair of the wizard's staff — "

"Oh, yes, but — " Fortnight hesitated.

Kane thrust his hands into his pockets and swung around to face for the first time that darker shadow which was the Samoan.

"So — was that a trick played by our side? Why?"

"We had to delay the *Sumba* at Jolo and plant a suggestion of foul play in van Bleeker's mind. Capt. Boone knows of the captain's stubborn nature. He thought that the captain should be placed in the proper mood so that you could influence him. It worked out that way, did it not?"

"So well that I wouldn't care to be around on the bright and sunny morning when it is all explained to van Bleeker. We have listened several times to his plans for dealing with the Guru if he ever lays hands upon the miserable worm. Dutch, Fortnight, is a perfect language in which to swear — ”

“Certainly, sir. But there is no need to ever inform Capt. van Bleeker of the inside workings — ”

“Of your plot? Ignorance being bliss. I suppose you won’t tell me just who doubled as the black wizard?”

“I was not informed, sir — ”

“All right. As long as he covered his tracks so well, he’s probably safe. I’ll keep mum. But *I* am not going to make van Bleeker the target for any innocent merriment!”

“Perhaps no such sacrifice will be required of you, sir. Capt. van Bleeker’s temper is co-operating with us very well now. And remember, sir, this is wholly between us — this — this — ”

“True confession session? Okay. Only Sam must be in on any future plans. He’s one of Boone’s bright boys too, you know.”

“Of course Sgt. Marusaki must be told. That is understood. Only it would be best for us not to be seen together any more than is necessary. The men of the *Sumba* are loyal to their captain. And they are also for the most part both intelligent and curious. Then there is the other gentleman — the Jonkheer van Norreys — ”

Kane snorted. “There you *are* off the beam, Fortnight. Lorens van Norreys has been playing our game for years — only on the other side of the globe.”

“Perhaps he has played it too long, sir — ”

“What do you mean?”

“Only what you yourself must have noticed, sir. The Jonkheer van Norreys has been living on his nerve for a long time. Such men are sometimes dangerous, to themselves and to others. The end comes in two ways — either they are burnt out, dead in spirit — or they lose all control and become chronic hysterics. Watch Your friend carefully, sir — ”

Kane rammed his fists deeper into his pockets. “I don’t believe you,” he said flatly. “Lorens may seem nervous, but when he is serious about something he changes, is more quiet and alert. I have seen him change when he faced both Lao and Hakroun — ”

“But still I ask you, sir, do not speak to him of our connection — ”

“I have no intention of doing so. Anyway the poor guy has enough on his mind now. Why break it to him that the war may not be over? What's your next move? Any orders from Boone?”

“None except to continue with the *Sumba* and do all we can to keep her sailing south. There may be further instructions waiting us at Besi.”

“All right. Good night, Fortnight.”

“Good night, sir.”

Kane crossed the deck. There were many shadows and little light, but the round eye of an uncurtained port-hole brought the American straight to the cabin he wanted. He tapped on the slatted inner door and was glad to hear, “Come in.”

Lorens was curled up on the lower bunk, several cushions under his head. As the American stepped in he laid aside the book he had been reading.

Kane regarded the dully-bound volume with a quizzical eye.

“Catching up on your homework?” He picked it up and glanced at the heavy print on the time-brittled page.

“In a way. Just looking up the legend of the Forbidden Place in the memoirs of one of the old sea rovers who explored these seas. Luckily van Bleeker has a taste for such literature and a collection of it in his cabin. The legend is here all right. An island of the golden age, with a genial despot for a ruler and all the wealth of the Indies showered upon its people. No illness dared to strike there, no evil fate invade its shores. But so jealous were they of their immunity from the common lot of the rest of the world that they would hold no commerce with outsiders, and they put to death all those who tried to come to them."

"And the truth of the story?"

"Perhaps some petty rajah found him an island and set up a court there. He might have gone to the extent of murder to preserve his sovereignty. Whatever the story was, it came to an end long ago. Only there *is* the Nararatna — "

"That's the third time you've spoken about that necklace. What is it anyhow which makes it so important?"

"It's a powerful talisman, about the most powerful you can find in the East, and its value is fabulous. It must always be constructed of certain precious stones set in a very definite pattern. The chain from which it hangs is the Mani-mala and is made thus — " On a slip of paper the Netherlander began to sketch. "Diamond, ruby, cat's-eye, pearl, zircon, coral, and emerald on the left as you face the wearer. On the right will be rock crystal, quartz, carnelian, garnet, chrysoberyl, sapphire, and topaz. From between the emerald and the topaz is suspended the Nararatna itself.

"In its center is the ruby which stands for the sun. Direct east is Venus, a diamond; southeast, the moon, a pearl; south, Mars, coral; southwest, Rahu, jacinth; west, Saturn, sapphire; northeast, Jupiter, topaz; north, the descending node, a cat's-eye; and northwest, Mercury, an emerald. Always the same pattern without change. And that one Hakroun showed us was very old. If it was taken from our trader and he brought it from the Forbidden Place — well, then I am wondering whether that island is one with Lemuria and Atlantis after all!"

8

SOELA LANDFALL

"How about a buffalo in your game bag?" Sam gave an extra swab to the stock of his rifle with the old silk handkerchief he dedicated to that honor.

"Buffalo — on an island this size — ?" Kane nodded shoreward at the long earthen finger which was Besi.

"Oh, even the buffalo came fitted for size hereabouts." Sam's cleaning equipment was going back into its box. "I'm thinking about the anoa — they stand about three feet or so at the shoulder and live in pairs rather than in herds. And you have to be pretty good at trailing before you're able to bring back their horns and hides."

Kane squirmed lower in the deck chair. "If an anoa or buffalo hunt means honest labor of any sort, you may count me out. This is no climate in which to go clambering around through a jungle. None of that for me — "

Sam's scorn was open. "You're getting fat, fat and soft! Wish Ironjaw could see you now."

Kane jerked erect — as erect as one can get in the grip of a pre-war deck chair. "Perish that thought and speedily. Why try to raise horrid visions? Hi, Lorens." He hailed the man coming up the deck. "Sam is panting to go buffalo hunting — are you in a bloodthirsty mood too?"

The Netherlander dropped down on the footrest of Kane's chair. "Not particularly. Should I be? This is a good day on which to do something though — "

"Lt. de Wolfe, the government agent here, has sent a message that there is a turtle hunter in port just now, and Capt. van Bleeker is going to smoke him out. Tortoise shell is a good investment. There is also a tierhander camping out in the guesthouse — "

"A what?"

Kane waved an admonitory hand at Sam. "Don't display your vast ignorance so plainly, chum. You mean one of those three-inch spiders, don't you? I've seen the permanent inhabitants of guesthouses in this particular corner of the world many times before."

"Hornhoven would not care to be referred to as a spider," observed Lorens. "No — a tierhander is a hunter, but he does not use weapons such as these." He patted Sam's rifle almost affectionately. "He uses nets and ropes and traps of his own devising. Live animals for circuses and zoos are his stock in trade. He may try to persuade van Bleeker to ship some of his current catch. And if the commercial aspects of Besi are as unrewarding as were Manado and Jolo, perhaps he can talk our captain into it. Then we shall head straight for Australia."

Kane's eyes met Sam's. "By all means then let Hornhoven fail in his hopes," both Americans were thinking.

"Do you believe van Bleeker would agree to that?"

"He needs the money which such a charter would bring," Lorens pointed out. "On the other hand such a cargo is unpleasant and difficult to handle. Then, too, our captain has a stubborn desire to defeat Hakroun, whom he now blames for his trading disappointments. You know what virtue the world accords my nation — that of stubbornness. We have a way of refusing to let go, even after all reasonable men would admit themselves beaten — ”

“And so you usually win,” Kane commented. “I’d say that was a useful virtue. What sort of a cargo does this tierhander have ready to ship?”

“You should ask that of de Wolfe — he is quite unhinged in his mind over the matter since twice specimens have broken loose and disrupted local life. There is a pair of your anoas, I believe, and some flying squirrels, black apes, and something of a large collection of snakes — ”

Sam got to his feet. “Hornhoven is not going to ship those on the *Sumba*!” There was iron determination in his voice, and Kane laughed.

“If they move in, you move out, eh? This sounds interesting. Does he allow visitors to inspect his catch?”

“As long as they don’t meddle with the cages. I have heard that he suspects part of his recent juvenile audience of loosing the apes twice. The trouble was, that instead of running into the brush, the apes went into the guesthouse and made themselves at home with Hornhoven’s most cherished belongings. One of them ate soap and foamed in the most suspicious way — there were several threats of shooting.”

“I think that a visit to mijnheer tierhander’s display is clearly indicated. If we are going to have them for fellow passengers, we should be formally introduced. After all, how can we tell, they may feel the same distaste at having to share traveling accommodations?”

Kane drew a long questing sniff as they came into the guesthouse grounds.

“Yes, monkey house in Central Park all right. What a mug *this* guy has!”

The occupant of the designated cage moved closer to

the bars, thrusting his face against them. He was studying his visitors intently, his protruding eyebrows arcs of
surprised interest. Lorens gave a little hoot of laughter.

"Perhaps he sees as little beauty in us," suggested the
Netherlander. "If he is considered a handsome specimen
of black ape, which he probably is or Hornhoven would
not have him here, we must seem masterpieces of ugli-
ness to him — "

As if Lorens had been entirely right in his surmise, the
ape snorted and withdrew to the center of his barred
domain. Selecting a fruit from a cache there, he began to
eat, turning his back on the outer world so that only the
long hair on his head, his hunched shoulders, and rud-
imentary tail remained in full view.

"Such rudeness!" Kane glared. "I'll never come and
see you in your future home. And you needn't think that
you're going to be a shipmate of mine either. Van Bleeker
will have a full report on *your* manners."

Sam had wandered on to a much smaller cage and was
now bent nearly double before it, chirruping to what
looked like a very untidy wad of brownish-yellow knitting
wool someone had negligently stuck into the fork of a
branch.

"This thing's asleep or something," he said as the
other two came up. "What is it anyway?"

It was Lorens who identified the exhibit. "That's a
tarsier. Clever little chap. But he always sleeps in day-
time. He lives in trees and gets around as a sort of combination squirrel and monkey."

"If he sleeps all day I don't see what good he is going to
be to a zoo. Who's going to sit up at night and watch him
do his stuff? Whee — what a stink? The grandfather of all
skunks must be in here!" Kane, dismissing the uninter-
esting tarsier, had gone on to its neighbor. "Glory be, it's
a cat!"

"Malay civet really. Looks more like a fox about the head, doesn't it? They can be tamed — "

"Not as long as they smell like that," Kane interrupted.

"Ho, do I have visitors?" A tall man, a thick mat of reddish beard across his wide chest and a Malay turban twisted about his head, came down the path between the cages, walking with the quiet tread of a trained woodsman.

"Mijnheer Hornhoven?" Lorens held out his hand. "Hearing of your collection we took the liberty of coming to see it. My friends are new to the islands, and these animals are the first of their kind which they have seen. We are off the *Sumba* — "

The tierhander shook hands vigorously with all three. "This is good, heeren. You have come to see your future shipmates, ja? It is my hope that Capt. van Bleeker will take pity on me and let me ship them on the *Sumba*. The freighter I chartered is now two weeks overdue, and since we have had no message from her, I am beginning to fear the pirates have gobbled her up."

"Pirates?" Kane broke in.

"Ja, pirates! Within the past six months five ships are gone. Like that!" He snapped his fingers. "And all in the southern waters. Not big ships, you understand, and not government or European ships, only large praus or native-owned craft. Mine was a Chinese trader. So she is gone too."

"Storms, reefs, floating mines," Lorens suggested.

"For one or two such disappearances, I would answer ja — but not for five! Five is too many to vanish because of such natural causes. So do I hope that the *Sumba* will take my cargo. When van Bleeker finds his turtle hunter then perhaps he will have time to listen to me also. But while we are waiting upon that happy event let me show you my treasures! For I have treasures here, indeed I have. And zoos which have lacked fresh blood now for six

Sword In Sheath

years will be glad to see them. The market is goedt, very goedt! Come, heeren, this way, if you please. Apes, civet, tarsier — they are — as the Americans are so fond of saying — 'old stuff'. Here is my new stuff."

The line of cages to which he led them was a shorter one. Sam glanced into the first, then stood still, an awful sort of fascination mirrored in his eyes. Matching him stare for stare was a lizard, reared on its hind legs in a man-like stance. It hissed, and from its light brown shoulders expanded a nine-inch frilled ruff of orange-yellow speckled with red, as if gouts of fresh-spilled blood winked there.

"Good Lord! A miniature dinosaur!" exploded Kane. "And it must be more than two feet tall too!"

"A variable lizard, mijnheer. And it is large for its kind, being about two-and-a-half feet by your scale of measure. These run on their hind legs when pursued, and the natives say that when so running they can actually cross a stream by striding on the surface of the water. But that I have never seen. Ja, he looks a proper devil, that one, does he not? But it is more bluster than fight; he is out to scare you with his ruff and his hissing. Be still, devil one." Hornhoven tapped the netting across the cage front, and the lizard went down upon four feet, its frill falling in dull folds across its neck once more.

"And here are the snakes — "

Sam came on with the rest but only because of iron determination. He forced himself to look into each box, look as long and as intently as did his interested companions. But there was a wet shine on his dark skin, and the corners of his mouth deepened into tight gashes. Kane took pity on him and hurried their pace as much as he could. To tell the truth, the coiled occupants of the cages were none too pleasant sights, though he could understand the enthusiasm of the tierhander as the man pointed out the beauty of scale pattern and the grace of movement displayed by the captives. But to Kane, as to Sam in a greater degree, there was something both alien and very ugly in the fluid grace of the swaying rope bodies and the narrow uplifted heads.

Now the turtles were different, and Kane hung over the pen at the end of the reptile line engrossed with the huge hawksbill monster slumbering there. It looked both wise and old and even rather comfortable, dozing in the shade that way. Hornhoven explained that it had been bought from the same turtle hunter van Bleeker was now hunting down, and that its kind were common enough. Only the shell formation on this one was oddly patterned, and the tierhander believed that it would bring a fair price.

"Now that you have seen my little pets," Hornhoven boomed as they turned away from the last pen, "you will perhaps speak for them to your captain. To stay here is for me to waste money. Twice have those little native brats opened cages and turned loose my apes, causing much damages and for me making much trouble. If I never see Besi again, yet will I be happy. That Lt. de Wolfe, he was goedt against the Japs. Ja! Getting out to the hills and fighting them at all times. But he has bad ideas for business and trade. So him, too, I will be pleased not to meet too soon again. You will join me now in drinks, ja? This way — "

Again they were borne along by Hornhoven — this time to the wide veranda of the guesthouse.

"Ho, Jambi, do you bring out that American drink for the Tuans!"

Jambi, with a vast and beaming pride, brought forth two bottles of Coke and measured an equal portion into three glasses. Hornhoven watched the transaction jealously, then said, "Brought those from Singapore, I did. Got them from an American steward. He told me that is the most popular drink of your country. He was right — ?"

Kane sipped the un-iced drink. "It is. And this *is* a treat, mijnheer. Not much of this south of Manila, I imagine."

The big man chuckled happily. "And now" — he put one hand in the unbuttoned front of his damp shirt and brought out a small cotton bag — "to business. You are," he addressed Lorens, "a buyer of gems, de Wolfe said?"

The Netherlander nodded, and Hornhoven inserted a fat forefinger and a broad thumb into the minute bag. When he withdrew them a gleaming bead was tight in his grasp. This he rolled across his palm lovingly before he held it out to the younger man.

"How much is that worth now?"

Lorens held it up to the light. It had, Kane saw, the luster and fine glow of a pearl, not white, not cream, not yellow, but a very faint rose. But it was not a perfect globe — instead it was an oddly shaped piece, not unlike a small monkey head.

"Baroque," Lorens said. "The luster and color are very fine. Were this a sphere it would be worth a fortune, but in that shape the price would be small."

Hornhoven shrugged. "Ah, well, I never thought to make money easily. With me pennies come the hard way. No value — to me it has. It is a little monkey face, so plain, see? I think that I shall have it set into a ring maybe. For me it might bring luck. I am a man who would attract monkeys."

"Where did you get it?" asked van Norreys almost idly. "I thought that I knew all the texture of pearls from these waters — that rose color is new — "

"I bought it from that turtle hunter, the same one who sold me old Augustus down there in the pen. And he found it himself — or so he told me."

Lorens' grasp on the glass of coke tightened. He lifted it to his lips, but Kane doubted whether he tasted the lukewarm liquid.

"Found it! Did he chance to say where?"

"Do you think that I did not ask him that myself — many times over? He was evasive, was that hunter. But then I know little of pearl fisheries. Perhaps a more knowledgeable man could get some useful hint out of him. But mind you, Mijnheer van Norreys, if you make your find you should remember old Hornhoven — "

Lorens grinned and unfolded his thin body. But before they could make the proper polite farewells, Hornhoven sent a roaring order into the darkened interior of the guesthouse, and Jambi reappeared, in his hands a belt of dark hide and a scabbarded knife. Hornhoven slipped the belt through his coarse fingers and half drew the knife from its sheath. It was clear, blue-tinted steel, and Kane's fingers itched to touch it. But the tierhander offered belt and knife to Lorens.

"Such a weapon as this you will not see elsewhere. That belt and the sheath are made from the hide of a komodo lizard — those monsters from the early days who yet live in the islands. And the knife came from the forge of Damascus, or so the liar who sold it to me swore upon the head of his father. Take it, boy, it is yours."

"But why — ?"

"Why do I give it to you? For two very good reasons, Mijnheer van Norreys. One" — he held up a forefinger — "I went aboard the prau of that turtle fisher when first she made port here. On her deck were fresh scars, and I have seen the paths left by bullets too often to be fooled. Then she carried too small a crew for her size. Something happened on the voyage from which she returned, something which her captain did not see fit to tell me or Lt. de Wolfe. And second" — another finger joined the first — "when I was new come to the islands I had two bad seasons, one after the other. A ship was lost and with her two black leopards and a python, which meant a lean purse for me. Then I came down with the fever, and that was very bad indeed. I had no funds left at all.

"There was nothing in the future for me but to beg passage home from the government — that, or to sink to caging and doing those things a European does not do in the islands, does not and keep his self-respect. And I was young with much pride. So one night I took from its case my gun, and I will not say what thoughts were in my head. No, not to this day do I like to remember those hours. But that same night a man came to my hut. He was a big man in the Indies, so big that his word was law im many places. And he made me a proposition. He wished to try a new trade, a trade in snakeskins, he said. And he wanted to back me in an expedition to gather them.

"From that hour my luck turned. But it was not until long afterwards that I knew that my employer at that time had no more use for snakeskins that he did for four arms. And if he had needed them, his own men on the islands would have supplied him gladly. No, he saved me, as he did others.

"So I had this made for him, but when I went to deliver it I was too late; he had left Java, sailed for home. I never saw him again. But it gives me happiness now to give the Jonkheer's gift to one of his blood. You may find it useful if you go pearl hunting — especially in these waters. No, don't thank me, Mijnheer van Norreys. Now go and hunt your fisher of turtles. Be off with you!"

"Your grandfather," Sam observed, as they walked back towards the shore, "must have gotten around a lot in these parts."

Lorens had pulled the knife from its sheath and was trying the edge on his thumb cautiously. "He lived in the Indies for more than thirty years, and most of the older traders and residents knew him. This is a wonder — " He balanced the blade on his palm, then, with a movement almost too swift to follow, threw it. Ten feet away a quiver of icy light appeared in the trunk of a tree.

Sam's breath went out in a whistle of admiration. "Smart trick. I thought only a Mexican or an Indian could do that."

"One learns such things." Lorens ran ahead and pulled out the knife. Wiping it carefully he restored it to the sheath. "I have had training in an odd school during these past few years — "

"So have we," returned Sam quickly. "There are things one can do with a bit of sharp bamboo now — "

"Shut up!" Kane interrupted. "I don't care to remember," he continued sharply, "the things one can do with a piece of bamboo — none of them are pleasant. What about it, Lorens, think that this hunter has found your new pearl bed?"

"Who knows. But the tint of that baroque was new — which means a different bed from any I have seen specimens before. A pearl man can tell from the color the general waters from which the gem was taken. And I had good training — the best in Holland. New color usually means a new bed. We can only ask."

"What about those fresh bullet scars Hornhaven mentioned?" Sam wanted to know.

"Maybe the guy met up with the pirate. Anyway, let us hope that van Bleeker won't make a deal which lands us on the same ship with that ape and a bunch of snakes!"

Sam shuddered, and not altogether in mockery. "Monkeys are bad, and that civet does not resemble attar of roses — but snakes ! No, please, no snakes!"

"No legless ones anyway," agreed Kane. "But the two-legged variety may still pop up in our path — "

"Yes, wearing head scarves and waving cutlasses. That is what regulation pirates wave when they board ships, is it not?" Lorens smiled. "I have always wanted to fight pirates since I read of Long John Silver — "

"And his parrot, Captain Flint," chanted Sam. "Well,

Sword In Sheath   **103**

boarders away and beat to quarters! Here we go to sweep the Main, my bully boys! 'Fifteen men on a Dead Man's Chest — ' " He broke into a song which brought up in silent amazement a party of Besi natives market bound.

9

DEATH PADDLES AN OUTRIGGER

"**S**ee" — Sam threw out his hands in the exaggerated gesture of a stage magician — "no snakes!"

Kane sniffed the sea air. "Nothing else either. So van Bleeker decided against the zoo?"

"No, the zoo decided against him — at the last moment," Lorens explained.

"Oh? And why?"

"Well, there was a promise of another perfect pair of anoa being brought down from the hills. And Hornhoven succumbed to the temptation of waiting for them. Also, the *Sumba* has acquired a shady name, and two of his handlers flatly refused to sail on her. But van Bleeker made a deal with the turtle hunter and has a fair catch of tortoise shell for his visit here."

"And the hunter — did he talk — about pearl fishing and bullet scars, for instance?" Kane inquired.

"Not yet — "

"Not yet? Well, if he talks now it won't do us much good. Besi is about a day behind us, and he'll do his speech-making to palm trees or Hornhoven's apes — "

"I think not" — Lorens was smiling — "since he sailed with us. Last night was rather hot — remember? And I thought a breeze might be had on deck. So I was up here in time to witness a strange sight. Our friend the turtle hunter was being persuaded to come aboard — by your Samoan, Fortnight!"

"Fortnight — Fortnight was bringing him on board?"

"Rather say dragging him," Lorens answered. "He was limp and something of a problem to manage. Yes, Fortnight brought him aboard. Mate Jasper seems to possess a goodly amount of muscle. And now, Lt. Kane, just who do you think you are deceiving?" Lorens' voice remained light, almost mocking.

Kane blinked and Sam's grin was erased.

"Suppose," continued the Netherlander casually, "we no longer occupy ourselves with what you Americans call 'fun and games'. Why did you order that man brought on the *Sumba*? Van Bleeker might like to know the answer to that question also — "

"But I didn't order him brought on board!" Kane exploded.

"Now, now, lieutenant — "

"I'm not a lieutenant! I've been out of the Army for almost a year — "

Lorens was still smiling gently, but beneath that smile was a quiet intentness. "Do you know — your vehemence almost convinces me. But then, why is Mijnheer Fortnight so busy a bee? I find his efficiency even more disturbing when it is not a product of your orders. Who is Jasper Fortnight? That question begins to intrigue me. I like mysteries, and this one is most providential; it gives my mind a bone to gnaw upon. Only maybe van Bleeker should be allowed to play too. After all, this is his ship, and he is responsible for Fortnight being on her — "

Kane wet his lips.

The Netherlander laughed. The sparkle of excitement was awake in his eyes. "I will not tell van Bleeker immediately. But on one condition only, my friends. You must make for me a place in this game you are playing. I am not green at it. Two years and more have I played it, too — with my life as the stakes. And now I discover that I have not forgotten the moves. Only you had better keep the captain from discovering what is going on aboard the *Sumba* — if you can. Van Bleeker might be seriously annoyed — as he has a right to be."

Before they could answer, the Netherlander got to his feet and strolled away. Sam muttered a comment which Kane interrupted.

"Yeah, I can see that — he's leaving so we can call in our third conspirator. And that's just what we had better do. What is Fortnight up to, anyway? You take port side, and I'll drift along starboard, and we'll see if we can find that guy. He has some tall explaining to do. But don't you go asking questions too openly — "

Sam snorted. "Listen, Dutch, I've done this little chore before. Only now I'm beginning to think that we must have signs pinned on us in some prominent place — signs reading: 'Look out. Undercover man at work'. And we thought we were so good!"

"Listen — you play 'now-you-see-me-now-you-don't' with the Gestapo for several years, and get away with it, and you're not just good, you're darn near pefect! Van Norreys has probably forgotten more of this game than most O.S.S. men ever knew. If we can just keep him amused at our antics, maybe he won't gum up the works by going to van Bleeker. On ship the captain is absolute. He could clap us in irons; we'd have no come-back at all. Also I want to have a good talk with Fortnight — if he's going to pull tricks such as this he ought to warn us first!"

With sharp annoyance for a goad Kane started along

the deck as Sam departed to work the opposite side.
There were plenty of the crew in plain sight. Everyone in
fact — except the tall Samoan.

"Lookin' for someone, son?"

Chief Bridger, a dark mustache of oil disfiguring his
pink face, was watching the American with lively curiosity.

" 'Course you may be jus' takin' your mornin' consti-
tutional. Only it's a mite hot for that, don't you think?"

Kane came over to the rail. "If it's hot up here, what's
the temperature down in your department?"

"Hellish, strictly hellish. An' I don't mean no swear
word by that there either. Me, I'm used t' it an' so's most
o' my boys. Got one big buck who can tell th' right head o'
steam by laying his hand right on th' metal — that's a
fact! That'd cook th' skin right offen you or me now. But
he can do it. In some ways they're a darn sight tougher
than we are. Yet they get together nights an' gab 'bout th'
Demon Huntsman an' such an' near shiver their guts
out — "

"Who is the Demon Huntsman?" Kane spurred the
talker farther away from awkward questions.

"The Demon Huntsman. Oh, one o' them island gods
or devils like. He hunts down th' souls o' men with his
dogs. You have to git you a good anting-anting to git th'
best o' him!"

"An anting-anting is a lucky charm, isn't it?"

"Yeah, like a rabbit's foot or some such truck. Not that
I'm denyin' there's somethin' in this magic stuff. Now I
had my future told wi' th' maize kernels once — regular
old witch woman she was what told it too — an' she said
I'd come nigh to death with fire an' water but good
would come o' it after. An' it wasn't six months later that I
was on th' *Carrie O.* when she was torpedoed — that was
fire all right, all right. She went up like she was oiled. An' I
went int' th' water, which brought me on th' *Sumba*

where I've bin ever since. Yeah, that there fortuneteller, she knew her stuff. But th' rest o' it — demons an' th' like — well, I gotta be shown one o' them 'fore I take oath he's true. How you comin' wi' your man hunt, son?"

"So-so. Everybody admits that there are islands where a man can be forgotten — and then they turn a-round and say that there is probably no one there. So we'll just keep on going — "

"Like the *Sumba*, eh? Anyway the old man got hisself a piece of luck at Besi. That tortoise shell was prime stuff. Maybe that'll break th' hoodoo an' we'll do well from now on. We'd better! This is th' old man's last chance; he shot th' works fittin' up for this voyage. Who did you say you was lookin' for this mornin'? Couldn't be that Fortnight guy, could it?"

Kane gave up. "As a matter of fact, I was. Have you seen him around?"

"Th' old man put him t' work in th' tradin' room, fixin' things up ready for when th' natives come aboard t' see what we've got t' offer. He bunks in there too an' I guess he likes it. You don't see him moochin' around much. Want I should show you — "

Kane shook his head. "No, thanks. Capt. van Bleeker pointed out that cabin when we first came aboard. If you don't mind, I'll drift along there now — "

"Not at all, not at all, son. See you later — "

The slatted door of the cabin was tightly closed, but Kane, having rapped loudly once, bore down on the latch. Somewhat to his surprise it clicked open, and he stepped over the high sill into the rather dusky interior.

"Mr. Kane!" Fortnight was there, rising up like a jack-in-the-box from behind some packing cases. "Were you looking for the captain, sir?"

"No!" All the exasperation of the morning was in his outburst. "I'm looking for you! What in blazes do you mean by bringing that turtle hunter aboard this ship?

Have you gone completely crazy?"

Fortnight swung around the boxes. "Please, sir, do not speak so loudly. How did you learn that I — "

"How did I learn it? How did I learn it — Why, van Norreys witnessed your whole performance!"

"But — he said nothing — "

"No. He thought you were acting under my orders. And I haven't spilled anything to him — either. He just used his brains, they're good ones. He wasn't an underground leader for nothing, you know. But van Norreys is asking questions now, and he isn't the only one. Chief Bridger seems to have a few suspicions too. And only the Good Lord knows what van Bleeker is going to surprise me with — "

"Well" — Fortnight leaned back against the crates — "we couldn't have hoped for a much longer run. The crew of the *Sumba* think for themselves and — "

"I don't care about the crew of the *Sumba*!" flashed Kane. "But where is this turtle hunter and why did you drag him here? You'll get us into a mess with van Bleeker, and he'll dump us on the next island. We won't be able to protest either!"

"I hardly think that the captain will do that," the Samoan was actually grinning. "Not while I have this cabin mate — " He jerked his thumb behind him and Kane crowded up to the wall of boxes.

Squatting behind them was a thin brown man whose clothes were certainly the worse for long hard wearing and who scowled most energetically back at the tall American.

"You see, the turtle hunter is not here on my invitation at all." Fortnight pulled a cigarette from behind one ear. "He made a bargain with Capt. van Bleeker to pilot this ship to a new island in the south. At the last minute, after having already received part of his pay, he decided that he did not care to sail on the *Sumba*. So I was sent ashore to — ah — persuade him. Capt. van Bleeker is losing his patience; his trading failures have worn the first skin from his temper. Unfortunately our pilot now refuses to do his duty. So I wouldn't mention him to the captain, if I were you, sir. He is most touchy on that subject."

Kane rubbed his damp face with his handkerchief. "I should think he would be — even down here they must have laws against kidnapping. Van Bleeker must have lost his mind to try a trick like this. What are you going to do with him now?" He eyed the reluctant pilot with extreme disfavor.

"Persuade him to do his duty, sir. Some further argument will doubtless lead him to reconsider his decision — "

"Argument?" Kane glanced with suspicion at the Samoan's fists.

"Argument," repeated the other smoothly. "This talks — loudly." He replaced the cigarette and pulled a coin from his pocket. Even in the gloom of the closed cabin the shine of gold was easy to identify. The turtle hunter saw it too, in fact his eyes never left that metal disc which Fortnight flipped from hand to hand. "The captain can pay well for what he wants — and in hard money."

Kane was forced to laugh. "Then I'll leave you to your persuasion. And may the best man win!"

Fortnight permitted himself a small smile of triumph. "You may congratulate me, I think, sir, in advance — "

No. I'll await results. Now I had better head off Sam. He's hunting you down also. If you can't be good — be careful!"

Fortnight digested the remark. "The very best advice, sir."

Kane closed the cabin door behind him. That was one mystery solved anyway. And if van Bleeker trusted Fortnight to the extent of setting him his present duties, they should have nothing to fear from the captain in the future. But was the master of the *Sumba* after trade, or had he heard of the pearl Hornhoven had bought from this same hunter? A new pearl fishery would probably be worth a lot more than a trading voyage — especially with an expert, such as Lorens, on board to value the stuff.

It suddenly occurred to Kane that he knew little about the mechanics of pearl fishing aside from the simple fact that one dives for oysters, then takes the pearls out of their interiors. Perhaps a little study on the subject would be fruitful and rewarding. Should he pick Lorens' brains for his store of knowledge — or see what sort of reading matter van Bleeker's quite extensive library might supply? But first there was Sam to be headed off.

That was easy enough. The Nisei was crossing the companionway, his sandaled feet making little or no sound on the well-scrubbed decking. At Kane's "p-s-st" he came up.

"It's all right. Fortnight brought the guy on board by order — from van Bleeker. He had signed up as pilot and then decided to forget all about it. So now he's cooling off in Fortnight's quarters. It's okay."

"Funny how things happen around here." Sam leaned back against the wall of the deckhouse. "I am visited by an odd feeling, at times, that we're missing something — not being included in the inner circle, as it were."

"Yes? The answer to that is to do a little circling on our own. What do you know about pearls?"

"Pearls? They grow in oysters. And some people are able to grow them on command. Then they're 'cultured' and not worth as much — "

"I've heard of them. Sort of a monopoly among the Japanese. Say — " He was struck by a thought which might explain so much. "D'you suppose that what Hakroun has hold of is one of these home-grown beds of trained oysters? Could that racket have been started down here during the war?"

"I hardly think so. A project such as that can't be kept secret. An expert can tell a cultured pearl from the natural one. There's no reason to be hush-hush. And the process is a lengthy one, requires a lot of equipment and a big staff to keep it going. I'd stake a good bet that the one Hornhoven showed us was the real thing. But that pink shade in the color — that's new. Before this most of the pink pearls came from the Arabian Gulf."

"If van Bleeker locates a new bed, can he cash in on it?"

"Search me. I don't know the laws they have down here. There must be some sort of regulations — such as there are in mining — staking claims or something of the sort. But an untouched bed — whee!"

"Like that, eh? No wonder they have that turtle hunter locked up. How are you at diving, Sam? We ought to get in on the ground floor — or the bottom of the lagoon — too. I could do very nicely with several hundred thousand or so to play around with."

"It's not as simple as that. And you don't find a pearl in every oyster, you know — "

"Oh, I'm not that greedy. I'll settle for one in twenty. Hello — What's that racket forward?"

There *was* racket forward — both shouts and orders. Seamen leaned over the rail while a smaller group busied themselves with the launching of one of the shallow draught scows which were the usual ship's boats of an island trader. Kane seized on Bridger.

"What's the matter?"

"Driftin' outrigger. See — over there! Someone in her too, only he's down — !"

In spite of the glare of the sun on water Kane was able to make out a narrow black shadow which rose and fell without direction on the thick green-blue waves.

"Lookout sighted her — said th' fellow was up then.

He sort o' waved an' then jus' keeled over."

"Survivor from a wreck?"

"Not in an outrigger. But this is far from land for one o' those. 'Less it was blown out in a storm. An' we ain't had any storms — "

The *Sumba*'s boat had reached the outrigger now and the single occupant of the native canoe was pulled limply into the larger craft which then bore back for the side of the freighter at a rate of speed which suggested that help was needed. Van Bleeker was on the bridge, his glasses trained on the boat, but waiting to receive the party below was Felder with the first-aid kit.

As the scow came alongside someone shouted for a sling. Kane and Sam crowded forward as a makeshift stretcher came up and over the rail.

The former passenger of the outrigger was a native with a shock of bushy black hair. A strip of dirty cloth was twisted tight, not about his loins, but around his chest, and it was as stiff as a coat of mail with a great blackish stain over which a fresh wave of red was slowly seeping. Save for this bandage his dark body was bare.

Felder squatted down beside the stretcher and tried to loosen the hands which clawed into the folds of the bandage. He managed to free one, then cut away the cloth. Kane blinked. He had seen wounds like those before — too many times.

"Submachine gun," half whispered Sam.

Felder dropped the end of cloth, his hand moved to the neck pulse, then he got to his feet.

"He's dead," the second mate reported to van Bleeker as the captain approached the group. "He was good as dead hours ago — even before he put that on." Felder pointed to the bandage. "There's no hope of surviving that sort of wound — "

Kane fought down past memories and an odd feeling in his own middle. He knelt down in Felder's place. Sam was right about what had caused that appalling tear across flesh and bone, there was no need of verifying that. But there was a glint of light from that other fist, the one still gripping the cloth. The American set his teeth and began working at the stiff fingers. One by one he forced them free, first from the edge of the bandage, then open so he could take what had been held fast against death itself.

It was a small glass phial, perhaps once fashioned to hold medicine. But it now contained a bit of some grimy fiber rather like cotton and was firmly stoppered with a dull gray knobby thing which was certainly not a cork.

Van Bleeker's hand was on his arm. "Come, and bring that with you!" the captain snapped.

When, trailed by Lorens and Sam, they reached the bridge and some measure of privacy van Bleeker spoke again, "Open it!"

It took hard tugging to bring the gray stopper out. But with that done Kane was able to twitch loose the fibrous stuff — and from the heart of the roll dropped three spheres of glowing light.

"Good Lord," breathed Lorens in a tone which approached reverent awe. "That I have lived to see those!"

Kane was cupping in his palm three perfect pearls.

10

NOT ON THE MAP

"Three times nine is twenty-seven," van Bleeker muttered. "Twenty-seven like those — !"

"Twenty-seven!" Kane goggled down at what he held. "There're only three."

"You don't understand," Lorens cut in. "That diver was from Borneo, and there they believe in the old superstitions. Every ninth pearl they find is put into a bottle with two grains of rice, the stopper being made from a human finger bone. After certain incatations the pearls are supposed to change the rice grains into gems of equal value. So, if this man was true to the old customs, three pearls in the bottle mean that he had found twenty-seven to begin with. He was diving in a rich and practically untouched bed if he was able to find twenty-seven like those."

"The question being," pointed out Sam, "where did he come from? Are there any islands near here?"

"Not marked on the chart, no. How long, Felder, could he have lived with that wound?"

The slim, dark-faced young officer raised his shoulders in an exaggerated shrug. "How can any man tell, Captain? Those natives have great powers of endurance. The first blood on the bandage was dried, and he must have died just as our men reached him. Three hours, four, maybe more since he was shot. And who knows whether he was just now coming from the pearling bed? He might have brought those up months ago in a very distant place."

"I think not," Kane interrupted. "Suppose he was trying to escape from somewhere — maybe last night. He was shot at, made it to the outrigger, and pushed off — Couldn't a current have pulled him out here?"

Van Bleeker hunched over the chart table thumbing a hastily unrolled map. Felder had caught some of the captain's fever and was working out his own calculations.

"There is a drift, sir — " the Eurasian ventured. "Southeast — "

Van Bleeker stabbed the points of the dividers into the map.

"Southeast shall we try then. But with caution, you understand. And, Felder, take the keys to the gun locker and break out the arms. We have no wish to share the fate of this poor devil."

The *Sumba* changed course and sailed on. Upon her deck men worked to enfold in canvas the body of the diver, sewing the stuff smoothly about the pitiful form. And van Bleeker came forward when they had finished to read over that narrow bundle the words of the burial service. When it slid overside into the green depths Kane knew a queer feeling of loneliness. They would probably never know the name or history of the dead man; he would become just an entry in the ship's log, to be reported to the proper authorities when the *Sumba* made port again — if she ever did.

Now why should that thought cross his mind at this

time? There was no reason for the *Sumba* to run into trouble. Well armed and manned, the freighter could stand up against anything now cruising these waters since there were certainly no enemy subs or destroyers out — the war was over. Only those wounds — submachine guns were not the usual weapons of peaceful men.

"Land ho!"

The lookout's cry rang down to deck, bringing out passengers and crew alike. Kane hurried to the bridge to find as many of the watch as possible lining the starboard rail, glasses to the eyes of those lucky enough to grab them first.

"I don't see anything!" The American was openly disappointed. Lorens held out his binoculars.

"Over there. It's just a line across the water now."

But the line across the water grew taller until it became a hump of rough mountain climbing out of the sea. The *Sumba* proceeded cautiously forward at a reduced speed. Van Bleeker had no mind to pile her up on some uncharted reef. Because this sea-borne mountain was not on any of the maps he had routed out from their cases in the chartroom.

Below the crew was busy about one of the landing scows, and Kane saw three men come along the deck, submachine guns balanced across their arms. Felder stood by the linesman in the forepart of the ship, and his clear reports of the bottom came up easily to the little group on the bridge.

Van Bleeker put down his glasses at last with an air of decision.

"Part coral, part volcanic, I should say. Which may mean a lagoon. We'll cruise off here and send the boat in to leeward where there might be an entrance. Order it away now, Mister," he said over his shoulder to the ever-silent first mate, a Malay-Chinese. "Tell them to keep clear of land, just take soundings and find us an anchorage."

The mate touched his cap and was gone. Then the boat was swung over and men slid down into her. Kane padded away to his own cabin, only to discover that Sam had beaten him to it and had already taken out the Reisings.

"Expecting resistance in force?"

Sam shook his head. "Only being prepared. You saw what that diver got. I'm not asking for a sample of the same — if that is what the inhabitants of this beauty spot are handing out to one and all. Jungle up and down that mountain — we could use some barrage to soften it up before we hit the beach — "

Kane grinned. "And where are you going to get the big guns for that? No, we 'does' this strictly small style, we 'does' — "

"And I never did like tramping through jungles. I suppose we're to go in on the first wave?"

"Yeah, regular shock troops. Only no fruit salad on the chest afterwards for this little job."

"Who wants a battle star when he can get one of those pearls?" countered Sam. "All set? Then let's go."

They tramped back to the bridge. But Lorens was there before them. He wore the lizard-skin belt Hornhoven had given him, but now it supported the holster of a Luger. And, as he turned, the shirt flattened across his shoulders so that an outline stood out clearly beneath the thin cotton stuff. Kane glanced for the second time at that tell-tale bulge. A knife in a collar sheath — he'd bet even money that that handsome pig-ticker Hornhoven had parted with was now riding comfortably between its new owner's shoulder blades. A collar sheath! Which told a lot about a man who chose to wear it. Lorens hadn't been kidding when he said that this sort of work was old stuff to him.

All they could do now was await the return of the boat and speculate as to why that green-clothed hump was not charted.

"Maybe it just bobbed up a short time ago," was Kane's suggestion. "Don't volcanic islands have a habit of doing that?"

"Overgrown with vegetation like that?" scoffed Lorens. "It is manifestly a volcano cone, yes. But there are no signs of recent eruption and with these coral reefs around it — no, this has been here a long, long time. It is well off the regular trade routes, and if it lacks fresh water and good anchorage it might well be unknown. You can see no trace of man along the shore."

"From here it all looks straight up and down — no room to perch a village," was Sam's comment. "At last, here comes that boat! Now we'll know when we can put in — "

Yes, Felder reported, there was anchorage on the leeward of the island, deep enough within the encircling arms of the reef. They had made soundings and were ready to guide the *Sumba* in.

So for the next hour the engine room telephone heated up with a barrage of orders, as the freighter edged through the break in the reef into a lagoon where a tiny strip of beach backed up against an upsweep of dense greenery.

The two Americans eyed that shore line dubiously.

"For mountain goats only — that must be close to a forty-five degree rise." Sam tried to measure with his eye the precipitous slope where bald rock showed now and again through the mass of vine, bush and tree.

"I don't know. If we come in from the corner of the beach— it doesn't seem to shoot right up there, more of a slope. And if we *could* get to the top we'd have a good chance to see the whole place. Sort of a bird's-eye view—

"Only we aren't attached to wings — even tin ones.

This begins to remind me strongly of the good old days in the Owen-Stanleys."

"At least it isn't raining. And we can't really tell what it's like from this distance. Wait until we get ashore before you start crabbing — "

But Sam had already turned his attention from the shore to the lagoon.

"Wonder if this is the pearl factory. Care to go down and look around a little?"

"Do you wish a run ashore?" Lorens joined them. "Capt. van Bleeker proposes to lead a party in person."

"Now why do you suppose we have our scout uniforms on? Sure, we've taken an option on the front seats in the first boat to push off — "

They weren't able to get the front seats Kane had mentioned so confidently, but they were in the shore-going party which pulled away from the freighter a short time later. And they were right on the captain's heels when van Bleeker splashed through the few inches of water to the white coral sand of the sliver of beach.

"It would take one of your bulldozers to break through this — " He waved toward the jungle. But the Nisei shook his head.

"No, it's not so bad really. In fact we can wriggle through right here. That's the stuff, Fortnight — just what we need for this job!"

The Samoan came ashore carrying bolos, two of them — jungle knives which had been designed to fight nature long before the Moros had learned to turn them against human flesh. Sam took one and gave it an experimental swing to test the balance.

The *Sumba*'s captain turned to Kane. "You have had experience in jungle fighting, you and Marusaki. Are you willing to try to get high enough on the mountain to find a lookout — if that is possible? Felder, van Norreys and I with the men shall round the lagoon. I need not warn you about taking care — "

Sam laughed. "Take care? This sort of a set-up is old stuff to us, Captain. When you've harried the Nips through as many birds' nests like this one as we have, you, too, can get a diploma in skulking. Well, Dutch, do we charge?"

They fell into the old single-file pattern, the lead man swinging a bolo. Oddly enough it was Sam, small and slight as he was, who kept the best pace, his regular swinging strokes falling with a rhythm which never lagged. For Fortnight, in spite of his strength, it was a hard task. While Kane, until muscles unused for months got grimly to work again, found it plain drudgery.

Not that it was just a woodhcopper's holiday. There were places where the native rock of the mountain had broken through the lush vegetation. And there progress was a matter of scrambling, digging in toes and fingers, scraping hands and arms on sandpaper-faced stone. At the end of twenty minutes Kane leaned panting against a convenient rock. His shirt was plastered to his aching body with his own sweat, one nail had been torn from a finger, and the feel of knife-edged lava was so deeply cut into his palms that he would never forget it. But when Sam started on again he was ready to follow.

Their second rest was beside a slide of tumbled rock where the rotting wood of imprisoned trees showed between stone and earth.

"Landslide, maybe even an earthquake" — Fortnight pointed out the evidence — "a long time ago. We had better go around this; there is still danger in loose stones."

But going around took time, a lot of it. And on the other side of the slide they were faced by a nasty bit of climbing up a ledge which narrowed almost to a crack as they advanced. It was then that the Samoan produced rope from a neat belt of it around his waist, and they tied themselves together.

Fortnight, in the lead, pulled himself up to a higher ledge, then jerked the rope to bring up the Americans. They hauled themselves over the lip of a wide cut in the mountainside, a cut which sloped gradually up toward the left. Here the overgrowth of green stuff was thin, and the Samoan stood up, examining the rocky breast of the mountain at their backs.

"Look here — and there also!" He picked away with the point of his bolo. "This is tool work — all of this. A road cut out of the rock!"

"Road — ?"

But it was true. Kane could see for himself the marks the other had cleared.

"But — why a road here?"

"To reach a city, a temple up above — who knows? But much work went into the making of this, a long time ago."

"How long do you suppose?" Sam was scraping the soil back from the ledge under them, trying to uncover the surface of the ancient way.

"A very long time. See, down there trees have taken root across this path."

Kane and Marusaki followed that pointing finger with their gaze. The old road wound down along the mountainside toward that portion of the island which lay on the opposite side from the *Sumba*'s anchorage. They could trace its curve for some distance before the jungle swallowed it altogether.

"Suppose we stay with it the rest of the way up," suggeted Sam. "It'll be a lot easier than traveling like mountain goats."

"If it hasn't been used for so long, the Johnnies, who may or may not be playing around with machine guns, don't walk it. So I vote yes." Kane looked to Fortnight, and the big man nodded.

"I have seen no signs of recent use. And it will make

our task easier."

It was still necessary to use the bolos now and then, but with better footing and no rock climbing they kept a faster pace until, upon rounding a curve, Fortnight jerked back with a cry of dismay, forcing the others with him to halt. When Kane elbowed himself forward again he was on the edge of a sheer drop, looking down into a cup of jungle hundreds of feet below.

The American jumped back. "What happened, d'you suppose?" If Fortnight had not been careful where would they be now — down in that mess below? The Samoan must have been sharing that mental picture of disaster. There was a beading of moisture around his hair line, heavier than any the climb had produced.

"Earthquake, I think." Sam was nearer to the break but looking up, not down. "It looks as if a big slice of the mountain just scaled right off here. Well, what do we do now? I had a feeling that this road was too good to last."

Kane had turned to the mountain wall. It seemed rough enough to offer foot- and hand-holds. And it was the only answer to Sam's question.

"Get out the rope, Fortnight," he said over his shoulder. "Here we go again."

Sam groaned and stooped to feel gingerly of the calves of his legs. "I charge time-and-a-half for gymnastics," he warned. "And have you thought, my fine feathered friend, that we shall have to come down again after we get up? All right, all right." He took the rope the Samoan was holding out. "I can see the darn thing. I hope I'm good at knots — if I swing out over that gulf I want to be pulled back again — by your strong and willing arms — "

"Trustful little squirt, isn't he?" Kane asked Fortnight. "Keep your feet where they belong, Sam. I don't intend to do any pulling at all — my arms aren't what they used to be — say about an hour ago. Next time we make one of these expeditions I shall be the one to mooch around on the sand looking for pearl beds — not a mountain taming hero. Allez-oop, Fortnight!"

The Samoan hung the plaited lanyard of his bolo around his neck and began to climb. The first hundred feet were comparatively easy. But after that Kane gritted his teeth, forcing himself to keep eyes only on the stone before him and move up according to the holds Fortnight called out as he changed his own. Through a cotton-dry mouth he managed to grunt out the same instructions to Sam. The strap of the Reising cut into his shoulders with a file edge, and he hesitated between each shift of holds to make sure it was properly balanced. How long it took them to creep up that bad stretch he never knew — it seemed to pass as a week of sun-filled days.

But it could not last forever, and they worked again into a piece of porous, weathered rock where holds were many and easy.

"Wait!" Fortnight's voice was hoarse with strain. "I'm going to circle left now. I think that I can see the edge of a plateau over there — "

So they crawled crabwise left, and Kane suddenly felt the tug of his waist rope.

"Come ahead — good footing here."

They were up, all three of them, and before them was a gentle slope leading down into what had once been the fiery core of a volcano. On one side, to their right, a large section of the core wall had broken away, perhaps in that same earthquake which had shorn off the old road. So now what lay below was a saucer of which about a quarter was missing.

There was some vegetation, brilliantly green. But the dense mat which formed the jungle on the slopes was missing. And here and there, among the trees and bushes, were tumbled heaps of stone which somehow appeared too regular to be the debris of nature.

Sam took the binoculars from their case and slowly swept the outer rim of this sky valley.

"There's the city." Fortnight pointed to the stone heaps.

"City! Up here?"

"Your city is here all right," Sam confrimed the Samaon's guess. "And across there is something very, very interesting. A temple, I think, and one still in good working order by the looks of the altar down front. Take a squint for yourself, fella." He pushed the glasses into Kane's hand.

11

SIVA'S FOURTH FACE

Kane swung the glasses in a short arc. Out of a spur of the cone wall, almost straight across the crater valley from where they stood, there leaped into full and lavish detail what was most certainly the entrance to a temple carved out of the rock of the mountain itself. Grotesque masks of forgotten gods and demons leered and frowned over the desolation they had once ruled. But years had weathered their elaborate headdresses and chipped their bold features.

From the wry-faced god at the apex of the dark doorway Kane's gaze traveled downward until — Beneath the sticky envelope of his shirt he knew again the familiar crawl of aroused nerves.

There was a falt stone block before that doorway. And on that block was heaped a mound of bright-skinned fruit and brilliant flowers. Both offerings were arranged in a pattern. The American passed the binoculars to Fortnight and unslung his Reising.

"Shall we go in from the left?" Sam was already edging

in that direction. "More cover over there."

Kane evaluated the crater's cover with that searching care which had been so laboriously drilled into his mind and body. "Left it is. But they've probably sighted us already — "

"The flowers are withering. They have been there sometime — perhaps hours." The Samoan returned the glasses to Sam. "Yes, to the left is best, sir. And it would be prudent, I think, to move as much undercover as possible."

"You don't think there is still a settlement *here* then?"

"No, sir. This may be a holy place, but I do not think that anyone lives in the cone."

They began their progress around the outer edge of the valley next to the swell of the cone wall. There was cover enough in the ragged growth of brush and the stone piles of the lost city to conceal a regiment, and as long as they exercised reasonable care, Kane thought that they might remain hidden from any worshiper or worshipers who had climbed to sacrifice at that temple in the sky.

It could not have been a large place, this stronghold of the crater valley, even in the days of its greatest glory. But it had been the center of a rather high degree of civilization. The intricate carving which patterned most of the larger stones had been designed and executed by artists. And the immense piles of such blocks suggested that they were the remains of quite large buildings.

"Do you suppose this was all one temple? There's a place in Java where a single one covers a whole mountain." Kane had paused to wet tongue and mouth with a sparing taste from his canteen.

Sam hunkered down before a block and ran his forefinger lightly over the bas-relief appearing there. "It's allied with Hindu stuff anyway. Look at this jolly old girl with all the fangs and the necklace of skulls. She's Kali —

I'll bet a fiver on it!"

"Kali!" Kane studied the open-mouthed female monster who was apparently screaming in insane fury at the moment when the unknown artist had chosen to immortalize her. "Isn't she the one who is the patron of those necktie boys — the Thugs? I don't think that I care to have her turn up here."

Sam's puzzled frown grew deeper. "I never heard of her being worshiped in the islands. She's not a very nice old lady — nursed smallpox germs and indulged in heart-eating and other quaint pastimes of a like nature. Maybe this was the headquarters of a devil cult — like those in Tibet where they do a regular business in black magic. Here" — over Kali's horrible grin he pulled a piece of vine — "let her be veiled — permanently."

"We can leave her to the lizards." Kane got up. "Time to move on, soldier."

It was a very short while later that they caught sight of the bottom step of a wide stairway which led directly up to the cave-entrance of the temple. As they stood for a moment behind a half-dead bush they heard the sounds of a scuffle from the shadows above. A small stone rolled down from step to step. Kane caught the faint click of Sam's gun coming into readiness. His own fingers tightened.

A muscular arm covered with grayish-black fur arose over the edge of the altar stone long enough for black fingers to close about a fruit and jerk it away from the pile. As the rest of the fruit tumbled out of the pyramid arrangement to roll off the altar, more hands appeared to grasp and grab. There came a banshee shriek of outrage and fury and two plump bodies popped into view, one in wild pursuit of the other.

Kane began to laugh helplessly as the apes tore twice around the altar, then disappeared into the interior of the temple. Fortnight stepped into the open and the

Americans followed him.

"Those boys wouldn't be playing around so free and easy if there was anyone here." Sam stated the obvious as he began to mount the stairs.

But at the door of the temple all three hesitated. In the first place, the sunlight of the crater world did not penetrate far into the cavern, and there was something about its dark silence which was not healthy. Kane investigated the carvings of the lintel. Here were demons in plenty — no pleasant faces at all. Sam's supposition might be true — this could be a temple dedicated only to the dark gods.

The silence was strong, a wall closing in upon them. Even the racketing apes had been swallowed up. There was not so much as an insect's buzz to disturb the brooding of the older gods. Earth and dust made a carpet within the door, marked only by the tracks of the fruit stealers. Apparently the worshiper who had brought the offerings had not entered the sanctuary.

"We ought to have a flash to go in there." Sam shifted from one foot to the other. "It rather smacks of booby traps and such — "

"Wait — " Fortnight ran lightly down the stairs and into the brush below.

"D'you suppose he's going back to the *Sumba* for a flashlight?" demanded the Nisei.

"Not to the *Sumba* but he's probably going to get a substitute. Wonder where in thunder those apes went. They haven't come out, and we'd still hear them if they were doing half-mile laps around the place — "

"Of course, there might be another entrance — on the other side of the mountain, say. Dutch, do you know who that is over the door — there?"

"The cheerful gentleman with three faces? No, I'm sorry, but my education has been neglected; he's a total stranger as far as I'm concerned."

"To be really correct he ought to have four faces, one

on each side of his head. That's Siva, and the face he has turned out to the crater is the face of Siva the Destroyer — which is his worst personality. I don't think this city ws a very nice place in its heyday — not a nice place at all!"

Kane, after glancing at several scenes pictured in lurid detail on the nearest wall, was inclined to agree with him. But the art studies were interrupted as Fortnight came back, a bundle of dry twigs and twisted grasses in his hand. He struck a match to his improvised torch as he joined the Americans on the top step, and holding it above shoulder level, he went into the darkness.

The place was much larger than the size of the doorway suggested. On either side they could catch only glimpses of the distant walls where, in paint and stone, devils sported gruesomely. There were double rows of pillars carved, like the walls, out of native stone, which led straight ahead. And between these the explorers walked.

Kane found himself tiptoeing to keep his boot heels from ringing on the pavement. Here and there in the dust were ape prints, and twice the wavering spoor of a snake wrote a curved message under their feet. But nowhere was there any proof that man had walked here since the sky city had been deserted. And always the silence hemmed them in — almost menacingly.

The avenue of pillars brought them to the foot of a dais or platform which had been fashioned of one huge block of stone. And on this was planted a gigantic figure which might have appeared in a nightmare. Not that it had a grotesque demon face, a skull necklace, or a severed human head in its outstretched hands, as had some of the other idols they had seen.

Instead it was of semi-human form with only the normal number of arms, legs and head. It was standing, one foot slightly advanced as if about to step down from its place, and it gazed serenely from large gleaming eyes down the length of the pillared corridor to the square of sunlight which was the opening to the outer world.

But the face —

"Devil!" breathed Sam softly.

The torch in Fortnight's hand wavered as the big man's grip shook, then steadied.

Kane looked from the face several feet above his head to the painting on the wall behind it. There was a difference, a great difference. The god before whom they stood had been made in a different age, by other hands than those which had carved this temple and embellished it with their own vile imaginings. He was older — and more evil. There was nothing of the beast in that calm, smooth-planed countenance. Siva and Kali were but the nightmares of backward children compared to this.

"No Hindu made that!" Kane spoke his thought aloud.

Fortnight raised the torch higher. The details of the body were plain, as were the folds of the cloak which half hid its nakedness. As the torch moved the eyes glistened as if the thing were alive and — watching!

"Rock crystal set in the sockets." Sam's voice was almost too firm.

"But where did it come from? Who put it here?"

"There were old ones in these lands before my people came," Fortnight answered Kane's demand, "and that was long and long ago. We found cities long deserted, statues of men or gods of whom living men knew nothing. These are old seas, far older than we can reckon. I think that this was found here by those who built the crater city. In it they recognized a more powerful representation of what they, too, worshiped, so they gave it due honor. But it is old — just as that for which it stands is very old — "

"I don't like it! It's not decent. A stick of dynamite under it would make the world cleaner. It has too much power — " Sam's voice rose.

"Why not — it is Power." Kane stepped back. "You can blow it up, if you want to. Me, I'd rather not touch the thing. And I don't want to look at it any longer either. There's something about those eyes — "

Sam's words became singsong. "Yes, they look into you, and all the little meannesses and small evils which are there are counted and made important and — right." He turned away from the dais abruptly. "Come away! It's not for us!"

Without answering they followed him to the left, away from the giant. And here on the floor the pattern of the ape's tracks was thicker, as if the animals had beaten a regular path in that direction for some reason. Mechanically at first, then with real interest they followed that web of tracks. And so they came into a corridor which must have once been a fault in the rock, enlarged by the work of man.

It led for a few feet straight ahead, then turned at a sharp angle to come out on a broad ledge hanging above the other half of the island. No better vantage point could have been found. Sam took out the glasses as Fortnight pinched out the torch.

Here the jungle did not seem so binding. To the left, at some distance, there was a wide sweep of grassland, almost like an open meadow. Then, at the edge of a stream, the heavier vegetation began again.

"Caves!" The Samoan pointed eagerly to a series of dark openings, most of which were to the right and on a much lower level than the ledge where they now perched.

And there were marks against the mountain wall below those dark doorways, marks which could be seen even without the aid of the glasses. Some of the caves, if not all, were in use.

Not that they sighted any of the inhabitants. Perhaps they had taken to cover, which argued that the arrival of the *Sumba* was known and that the explorations ashore had not gone unmarked. The three kept close to the entrance of the tunnel at their backs, but it was rather like posing as targets in a shooting gallery.

"If we come around here" — Sam motioned toward the open land — "it will be easy going. Somehow I don't fancy storming up this mountain again — especially if there should be a hostile reception committee waiting somewhere along the way. They wouldn't even have to waste ammunition on us — there were several places back there where a couple of well-aimed rocks would do the business nicely. Well, do you think you will know this place again?"

Kane was searching the floor of the ledge for something which most certainly should have been there but was not — at least as far as he could see.

"Where did the apes go? There are no traces of them here, and yet we found plenty of tracks at the beginning of that tunnel — it looked as if it were one of their regular roads."

"We can look along the passage; there may be another opening that we missed." Fortnight touched a match to his improvised torch.

This time they scrutinized the walls carefully as they passed. And it was Kane who first sighted a pocket of shadow which betrayed the entrance to a sort of burrow. From it came a whiff of rank odor — like the scent which had clung to Hornhoven's animal pens. There were tufts of hair caught in the rough stone proclaiming it a passage in much use. But neither Kane nor Fortnight could attempt that door. Sam might possibly wriggle through, but since none of them knew conditions beyond, they decided against the risk.

"Torch is going." Fortnight held his concoction in both hands. "We'd better leave while it still burns — "

So their shuffle became a trot, past the dais of the Unknown, and it was there, almost as if a puff from between those stone lips had extinguished it, that the light went out. Running, they broke out on the steps.

All the fruit was gone from the altar now, save for a couple of badly squashed globes, the fleshy pulp of which made a feast for insects. But the old problem of who had placed it there held the three. Surely there must be some easier path up the mountain than the one they had found.

"Shall we swing around the other way?" asked Kane.

But there their luck was no better. Unless the worshiper had used the ape-hole, he must have appeared at the temple by magic. The ancient earthquake which had cut away the western wall of the cone had carried with it perhaps a quarter of the ruins, and there was only a straight drop down. After half an hour they found themselves back at their original point of arrival, having found no other path of descent.

"But there must be one," protested Kane. He smeared the back of his hand across his dripping face.

"Okay — so there must be one!" Sam still had energy enough to snap. "Unless these people sprout wings at will. Only we haven't found it. And if you think I'll go head first down that ape-hole just to satisfy your curiosity you're crazy! I might meet someone coming up. After all, Rome wasn't built in a day, and the *Sumba* isn't going to sail tonight. We can come up and try again. But now I vote we go back to civilization."

"Wonder how the shore party is getting along?"

Sam handed over the binoculars. "Take a peek. You ought to be able to sight them from that eagles' roost up there."

Kane clambered up on a pinnacle of rock and turned the glasses on the shore line far below. It was several seconds before he focused on the captain's following. They were gathered in a tight cluster out on a finger of the shore reef. And they seemed to be busy, very busy. While he watched, one of the figures dove into the green lagoon.

"They must have found something. They've taken to diving!"

Sam was up beside him in one wild lunge, pulling at the glasses. "Let me see!"

"Someone just dived. Maybe they've discovered the pearl fishery — "

"I'm pretty good in water, too. Suppose we go down and volunteer a bit of help. After all, we got what we came up here for, a look at the other side of the island. And we know about the cave dwellers. So let's hit the down trail."

The descent was not as difficult as the climb had been. Fortnight turned the rope into a ladder across the worst parts, and they followed the curve of the old road as long as they could without running into territory which might be under the direct control of the cave people. Panting and soaked with their own sweat, they came out at last on the same strip of sand from which they had departed hours before. Kane staggered down to dabble his hands in the wash of the waves. Salt stung his chafed palms and the cuts the lava rocks had made.

"Come on!" Sam tugged at him. "I want to see what they've found — "

The sand shifting under their boots was almost as hard to cross as the lava had been, and the coral was as rough as the stone. Those who were on the reef did not even look as the mountaineering party came up.

"Did you find pearls — ?" Sam was the first to reach the end of the reef.

A man stripped to his shorts, heavy diving goggles over his eyes, looked up at the Nisei. By his pale skin and blond hair Kane identified Lorens.

"There is an oyster bed, yes. But there is something else down there — wreckage!"

Kane edged over to peer into the murky water. The distortion of the undersea world was complete as far as he was concerned. Then a dark form spiraled up from the depths, and a native, wearing the same sort of goggles as those which made Lorens look like an insect, broke water.

"What kind of wreckage?" the American demanded. An illogical picture had formed in his mind. Why did that one word bring a vision of a Spanish galleon lying on its side with jewels dripping from every sprung seam of its weed-grown hull? He must have been conditioned by too many pirate stories in his youth.

"Metal of some kind." Lorens stepped gingerly to the edge of the reef and prepared to dive. "I'm going down to see — "

He slipped over and went smoothly into the dusk of the lagoon before Kane could answer.

"It is there, Captain." The native was making his report. "Tight in the coral trees it is. Big, very big."

"A ship?" questioned Kane.

"Tuan," the Malay answered him, "if it is a ship it is unlike any I have seen before, ever."

12

SUNKEN TREASURE

Lorens' head broke the surface, his water-darkened hair plastered to his skull. With even strokes he made for the reef and chose a landing place carefully before he climbed into the air. As he pulled off his diving goggles van Bleeker reached him.

"Well? What is it that that dunderhead Futa stumbled upon — a prau?"

The Netherlander was toweling his head with his shirt. "No. I think it is wreckage of a plane. The nose is wedged into a crevice of the reef, just as if she dove straight for that point. But a large part of the frame has been salvaged — "

"Salvaged!" Van Bleeker's voice ascended the scale. He glanced at the shore as if he expected to see a salvage party. But only the white-winged seabird wheeled and dipped and cried above the green twilight there. "By whom?"

Lorens applied the improvised towel to shoulders and upper arms. "By someone who knew his business. It is not a job done by natives. All that remains is that part of the fuselage which has plowed too deep into the coral to get at without blowing up the reef. I think that it is the remains of a bomber."

Sam was peeling off his clothes. "Suppose I go down for a look. Our job may have caught up with us at last — we were sent here to investigate lost bombers."

Lorens handed over the goggles, and Sam, stripped to his violently colored shorts, slid gingerly into the water. "Any sharks or other wild life?" he asked before he disappeared.

The Netherlander shook his head. "We have sighted none yet. But I see you wear a knife, that is good. It is well to be prepared."

To Kane the following minute seemed overlong. But then Sam bobbed up again, his grin wide and exultant as he made for the reef.

"She's a bomber all right, and one of ours, Dutch — or I'm a temple-haunting ape," he sputtered, almost before his mouth was clear of the water. "And she's been salvaged almost down to her ribs too. Which means — "

"Survivors!" Now it was Kane's turn to look shoreward. "But where have they gone? If I'd been holed up here for years, I'd have been down dancing on the beach when I saw a ship come in. And we haven't even had a hello. Are you sure that the natives haven't been scrounging the stuff? The metal ought to be worth something even in this backwoods."

"No." Sam was definite. "That job was done carefully by someone who not only was familiar with metal but who knew his way around a plane. He knew just what he was after, and he took it. And it's been down there for months by the look of it. Our castaways may have sailed from here some time ago — "

"Or met with accidents — fatal ones." Again Kane's

eyes went shoreward. "There is something about this island that is anything but welcoming — "

Lorens pulled his belt through its buckle. His eyes narrowed, not against the glare of the sun. "So you feel that too? Yes, there is something in the air of this place which is not good — not good at all."

Van Bleeker spat out an exclamation which was half impatience, half derision. "Superstition is it now? Should I provide anting-antings for the crowd of you? We can keep watch. We are men who are trained to use weapons, and we have them to use. I do not think we have anything to fear — we of the *Sumba!*"

"Doubtless you are right," conceded Lorens. "And" — he turned to Kane — "what did you find on the mountain top?"

Kane's tale of the ruins in the cone and the temple in the sky was so hurried that they stopped him often to demand details. It was the apes' passageway and the discovery of the ledge which was a vantage point over the other side of the island that interested the captain most.

"And you found no other road down?" he persisted.

"None — except the ape-hole. And that may not lead down at all. But there were no tracks of human feet in that temple. Whoever brought the offering hadn't come through there — "

"And even if we did find the path that worshiper used," Lorens pointed out, "it might not be well for us to follow it. The cave dwellers must know that we are here; they may have been spying on us constantly since the *Sumba* came into the lagoon. And we must be unwelcome — no one has come to see us openly. Remember what happened to that pearl diver?

"So an ambush on a trail would be only a routine move on their part. If we do invade the over-mountain territory, it would be best, I think, to cut around to the south through that section of open land which you noted. I have a liking for a fight in the clear myself. A skirmish in a mountain tunnel where my opponent knows the ground better than I do is not exactly to my taste."

Van Bleeker grunted, not more than half convinced. "Very well. First we shall try it your way — a frontal attack. Then, if we fail, we can once more attempt to find the mountain route. Back doors are sometimes easier to force than are the front — "

"Look here," Sam cut in, "everyone seems to be awfully sure we've got a fight shaping up — "

"All indications point to that." An air of tried patience showed through Lorens' usual courtesy. "We have not been welcomed — and there is the matter of the diver — "

"What if these people are only afraid of us?" argued the Nisei. "Lord, they may be the descendants of the old boys who built the temple. Maybe they've never seen white men or a ship such as the *Sumba* before. Hadn't we better find out how they stand before we go in with machine guns?"

"Maybe Sam's thinking is straighter than ours," Kane agreed, almost diffidently. "We've been fighting so long that perhaps we — "

"Have come to believe that force is the proper answer to every problem?" Lorens caught him up. "Yes, there is that. But, on the other hand, there have been stories of holdout Japanese troops and native agitators taking to cover on these islands. What better place for them to go to earth than a place like this, which is off the map? So I say, go armed, but let the other side declare their intentions first."

When they returned to the *Sumba*, Lorens went to work with a sheet of stiff paper and a set of drawing pencils to sketch a rough map of the island. With the sure hand of one who has seen it himself he drew in the reef and the shore line, then, more slowly, with Kane's awkward help and that of Sam's more supple fingers, the mountain and its crater of ruins.

"So here is your spy ledge — hmmmm — " Van Bleeker poked at the cross mark. "And here are the caves. How many of those do you think are in use?"

"We can't be sure — sure of anything," Kane countered. "But I would say that these" — he pointed at the map — "and these are used."

"Four here — three there. Big ones?"

It was Fortnight who answered that. "How can anyone tell from the size of the entrance. Many small holes open out into large caves. The cave of the temple is much larger than its entrance would suggest."

Van Bleeker chewed his thumb. "Then there may be a hundred or more living there — "

"Would this island support that many?" Kane wanted to know. "We haven't seen any fishing boats, and we didn't sight any large clearings under cultivation."

"Even ten men in caves such as those could make trouble for us. That back door now — if we could find that." The captain continued to pore over the sketch. "There — perhaps — "

"That's sliced off clean — The old earthquake path took a big hunk of the crater along with it," Sam explained. "That's what wiped off the end of that road which we found — "

"Yes, the road, I was forgetting the road." Van Bleeker's thumb went back to his lips. "But the lower end of that — it still runs into this bit of jungle here?"

"It must. Although we did not follow it past here. Only it would take a bulldozer to clean out that path; the jungle has grown clear across it. If we try to force a way through there we might just as well blow a bugle to announce us — we'd be as easily spotted in about five minutes!"

Lorens had his own answer to the problem. "We take the ship's boats to here." He made a neat dot of his own on the map. "How thick is this spur of jungle?" He looked up at Kane.

The American closed his eyes and tried to visualize the country as he had seen it from the ledge. There had been some greenery over to the south, but he could not recall how dense it had been — the caves and the land about them had held most of his attention then. "I can't remember."

"Not much jungle there," the Samoan supplied, "and not thick — not like on the lower mountain slopes."

"Good enough. So here we leave the boats and cut overland, which should bring us to this V-shaped point of the open country. After that we can keep to the slope, under cover of the brush most of the way long. The jungle does not begin again, you say, until you approach this stream?"

This time Kane could answer. "Yes, it begins at the stream. But even there it is not so dense — it isn't anywhere over there."

"Then that is my suggestion." Lorens waited for their opinions.

Van Bleeker still studied the map, reluctant to give up his own cherished project of discovering a back door. But with a final grunt he surrendered.

"All right, all right, then. Overland it is. But, mind you, this is no frolic for tin-medaled heroes. I think that we are going to walk into something nasty on the other side of the mountain. I do not like this — not one little bit. And when we go, keep to cover. We will have no death-and-glory charges in this — "

Kane clamped his teeth on a laugh. In place of van Bleeker's round chin and stubby nose he had, for an instant, seen the irregular angularity of Ironjaw's long face. At least their thoughts of battle were very, very similar.

"It only remains for us to decide when." Lorens rolled

up the map. "Tomorrow — before dawn — "

"Giving the inhabitants of this fair isle all night to set booby traps where they'll do the most good?" inquired Sam.

"It is not the easiest thing in the world to cross unknown territory at night, especially since we are not pushed for time — "

"Van Norreys is right," Kane said crisply. "And they can't be sure of our next move anyway. If they've been watching us, they know that we sent one party up the mountain and the other along the reef and shore. All right. How can they know that we plan now to march to the south? If their force is small they'll spread out so thin trying to cover every possible approach that they'll simply wrap themselves up in tissue paper and be a regular gift as far as we're concerned. And I don't fancy plowing through jungle in the dark when we've had no briefing about the route. I vote for a morning try."

"Okay, okay." Sam waved his hand in amiable agreement. "I'm no owl either. Morning it is then."

"And you, Captain?" Lorens turned to van Bleeker with that shade of deference he had always displayed toward the captain of the *Sumba*.

"Right enough. Before dawn it is. And who will go?"

"I think it is more a question of who won't," said Kane. And van Bleeker laughed for the first time.

"True enough. And, just in case there is a reason for these gloomy forebodings which seem to hang above our heads, I shall wireless to Besi the details of our proposed exploit. That will give de Wolfe something with which to occupy his idle moments. It may be that we have even discovered the headquarters of his pirates." The frown of concentration was back between the captain's sun-faded eyebrows again. "Which gives me to think — "

"What if this *is* the raiders' hideout and their ship or ships are at sea? Suppose that fleet comes in and bottles up the *Sumba*? That would not be good — not good at all!"

"How about asking the turtle hunter a few pointed questions?" Kane suggested.

"Yes, the turtle hunter." Lorens stopped making pleats in the edge of the map. "What has he to say about this island?"

But Fortnight was already on his way in quest of his prisoner. Van Bleeker appropriated one of Lorens' pencils and began composing a message designed to arouse and irritate the distant Lt. de Wolfe.

"How about it?" Kane asked Lorens. "Does this seem like a pirate stronghold to you? Not much activity to be seen — "

"There would not be — except when one of their ships was in." Lorens was drawing the outline of a prau on the pad of notepaper. "One of these now with the proper arms would be able to take almost anything now sailing in these waters — except, naturally, a regular war vessel. But, yes, perhaps we would see more signs of life were this a pirate port. I think that not even yet have we guessed right concerning this island — "

"But you did find pearls?" prodded Sam.

"We found pearl oysters, or rather, we saw them," corrected Lorens. "That may mean nothing. And on this side of the lagoon there is no trace of pearl diving. The answer to all our riddles must lie here." He unrolled the map and dug the soft lead of his pencil point into the location of the cave dwellers.

Van Bleeker poked the bell button on the wall at his elbow. And when the steward padded in the captain tossed a piece of much marked-over paper to him. "This to Jan and tell him it is for the Dutch commandant at Besi. There is no need to put it in code. And — here you are, Fortnight — does he wish to speak yet?"

Propelled by the Samoan's hand at the nape of his

neck, with Fortnight's other set of fingers gripping the waistband of his sarong, the turtle hunter entered the cabin with a total lack of ceremony and a semblance of haste he did not appear to find comfortable.

"He has not yet found his tongue. But I think that he will. If he does not, why should you keep a useless mouth aboard, captain? We can easily set him ashore — " began the Samoan.

The captive gave a broken wailing cry and grabbed for van Bleeker's hand. Missing aim, his fists fell to the table, and he gripped the edge of the board with a force that seemed likely to imbed his fingers in the wood itself.

"Not ashore — " he screamed, thrusting his dirty head forward, terror showing in his eyes while a thin drool of saliva twisted down his unshaven chin. "Not ashore, Tuan Besar, Noble Captain, Master of the Winds — Not ashore!"

Van Bleeker's lips curved happily. "Now I wonder why?" he inquired of the company at large. "Fortnight, you are right about useless mouths. We can do well without them — "

The man sank rather than wriggled out of the Samoan's hold. Still gripping the table, as if he were clinging to the one stable thing in a fearsome world, he collapsed to his knees. He wasn't even trying to deny Fate now, but he shook his head from side to side. A tear slipped down along his thick nose. Kane's stomach rebelled. It wasn't good to witness such fear.

"Why don't you want to go ashore?" the American demanded abruptly, for no other reason than to break through that curtain of abject, piteous terror.

But the turtle hunter was too deep in his personal hell — words couldn't reach him now. Kane moved, he wanted to stand up, to get around the table and shake that gibbering man into rational sanity again. A hand imprisoned his wrist in a steel grasp which held him in his place.

"We can get nothing from him now." Lorens' quiet emotionless words cut across the soft moaning cry of the native. "I have seen this before — he is mad with fear." Without raising his voice or changing tone from the same quiet pitch the Netherlander leaned toward the man and, releasing his hold on Kane, reached out his hands to put them over those fingers still biting into the wood.

"You are not going ashore, you are not going ashore. You are safe, entirely safe. You do not have to go ashore — " The sing-song of Coast Malay words made a pattern. Kane felt his own tenseness ebb away as he listened. "You are safe — you need not go ashore." The repetition was still quietly spoken, without color. But the head of the turtle hunter had ceased to sway in its horrible gesture of negation. His half-open mouth eased shut. Now Lorens' hands were moving, trying to straighten those cramped fingers, to loosen the man's grip. "You do not have to go ashore — "

The native's eyes fell to his hands and those others over them, then he looked up into Lorens' face. His mouth closed, he swallowed twice, then sniffed. Lorens spoke to the captain.

"Give him a drink. I think he will be all right now. But we had better not try that again. He was very close to the edge — "

Van Bleeker filled a glass and pushed it hastily in the general direction of the kneeling native and Lorens released the man's wrists. He looked to the Netherlander before he took up the gin and waited for Lorens' nod of permission before he downed the fiery stuff.

"Golly — " whispered Sam. "What in blazes *is* on shore anyway! That guy certainly had the wind up!"

"I think we had better find out," returned Lorens.

"I do not go ashore — " It was only a thread of whisper.

"You do not go ashore, you are safe," reassured

Lorens again.

The fellow actually smiled, grinned at them all, even at Fortnight who still blocked the exit from the cabin.

"Ask him what's ashore, maybe he'll tell you," Sam urged the young Netherlander.

But Lorens hesitated, almost as if he feared to hear what that answer might be.

"Do so." Van Bleeker's agreement had the force of an order. "We should know why this creature becomes a gibbering idiot when going ashore is mentioned. I have little liking for this — "

"Nor have I." Lorens' fingers were twitching a little. "He was mad with terror. If I should bring on such an attack again — "

"At the same time we don't want to walk into anything," Kane pointed out. "This may mean our lives."

"Or his reason." For the first time Lorens was bitter. "Very well." He began to speak in Coast Malay.

"Tell me — What danger lives ashore?"

The native was staring with a dog's intentness into the Netherlander's eyes.

"Danger ashore — " He repeated the words as if they had no meaning for him. Then a spark of intelligence flamed in his dark eyes, was alive behind his ugly face.

"Danger, much danger, Tuan. This is the Forbidden Place!"

13

SWEET POTATO DEDUCTION

"The Forbidden Place!"

"You still thinking about that?" demanded Sam from the upper berth. He might have meant his question jestingly, but the tone which echoed back from the roof of the cabin had something of annoyance in it.

"Just as much as you are, son," Kane returned cheerfully. "That's the umpteenth time you've turned."

"All right, all right! So I can't get to sleep. Well, I've heard you counting sheep also."

Kane folded his hands behind his head on the thin pillow and stared into the dark.

"Looks as if we can't take it any more," he challenged. "I don't recall these hysterics in the old days. D'you suppose we're getting old?"

There was a smother of relaxed laughter from above. "That may be it, at that. You know this has all the good old melodramatic ingredients of a pulp adventure story — a lost island with a ruined temple, that queer old god up in Siva's house, the mysterious bomber in the lagoon and the cave dwellers — All we need now is a bunch of bloodthirsty cannibals and the Marine Corps to arrive in the nick of time before we go into the pot. It's so much of an adventure story that it's funny."

"Yeah, only once in a while we run into real life. The turtle hunter wasn't amused by it all. That guy had it — bad."

There was a long moment of silence before Sam answered. Kane shifted on the tangled web of sheet and pillowcase. He didn't want to see etched across the darkness that terror-stricken face.

"His story was lame — even when van Norreys pried it out of him," Sam's words came at last. "All that stuff about camping out here, trading with two natives for pearls and then finding one of the fellows dead in the morning — "

" 'Torn, Tuan, as if some beast had been at him. But here, Tuan, I swear it to you — there is no beast of claws, no tiger — as all men know!' " Kane quoted.

"No four-legged ones, maybe," Sam corrected. "At any rate, he had the wind up — but good."

"You know — we may be talking ourselves into somewhat of the same state of mind right now," Kane said slowly.

"What!" But Sam's explosion was followed by sober agreement. "Telling ghost stories in the dark so we'll jump when the wind slams the door. I get it, partner. Okay — so long until tomorrow."

And the night hours were long. Kane sweated miserably in the dark. He set himself the old exercise of building words, a trick which had carried him through those bad hours before jumps, before attacks. One began with a noun and added certain adjectives and a verb until one had a sentence — each word must be seen in the mind, spelled out — defined —

"Up with you, sleeping beauty!"

Kane opened smarting eyes. It was a stinging slap which had brought him awake. Sam was thrashing about in the dusk, going through the movements of a contortionist while in the process of donning his clothes. Kane yawned and rolled over the side of the bunk, reaching for his slacks as he went.

"What kind of a day is it?"

"A fine frosty morning!" caroled Sam. "Just the type on which you'd choose to be shot. Come on, no need to beautify yourself today. We're businessmen, remember?"

"As if you'd let me forget. Do we get fed before this bold rally?"

"Always thinking of your stomach." Sam clawed impatiently at the cabin door.

"I'm part of an army, aren't I?" returned his companion reasonably. "And that's what an army travels on — its stomach. Sounds as if we were snakes or something of a like nature — "

Luckily van Bleeker and the *Sumba*'s commisssary were equal to the occasion. There were mugs of coffee flanked by well-filled plates on the mess table, and it did not take long to slide into one's seat and get to work.

"Van Norreys, Kane, Marusaki, Fortnight, Ali, Chang, and myself to go, Chief," van Bleeker was telling Bridger. "Shen and Felder will stay aboard."

"An' me?" The chief might be a plump middle-aged man in oily dungarees, but he was also loading a forty-five with a skilled touch. "Suppose th' boat sorta cruises around while you fellas go ashore? You might need some support — "

Both Lorens and van Bleeker reached for the map, but the captain got it first. And Bridger used the nose of the forty-five to make clear his suggestion.

"See, here's where you're goin' ashore, ain't it? All

right — suppose I take Kanake, Red an Bert an' ferry you over. Then we coast around this here point an' paddle along th' shore a ways. If you're goin' across clear ground like you say, then we can keep an eye on you — "

Van Bleeker consulted the map. "It is a good idea. What do you think?" he asked the others.

Sam shrugged, the rest nodded, without caring much one way or the other. It was Kane's guess that Bridger merely wanted to get in on the excitement and knew that cross-country travel was no longer for him. If it made the chief happy —

So now the scow which set them ashore in the dawn was crowded. They had pulled well away from the *Sumba* when Kane felt the soft touch of smooth and well-cared-for fur against his arm. A round head with pricked ears was silhouetted against the water. For some reason known only to herself the *Sumba*'s cat had selected to join the party. And when they reached the island she made the shore in a leap which her shipmates, splashing through water, might well have envied. Then she was gone into the high grass before she was seen by any except Kane.

Bridger and his men pushed the scow out again, and the shore party gathered in a sort of order. Almost instinctively they fanned out as they moved inland, keeping good space between each man.

The open land was not as easy to cross as it had looked to be from the mountain. In the first place it was overgrown with a tough and wiry grass, calf, thigh, and waist high, the blades of which had edges that could slash like bolos. So in no time at all they wore smarting scratches across hands and arms.

There were inhabitants in this grassy world, small things which squeaked and scuttled away from the invaders. And there were winged things which stung and bit impartially. As it grew light the party from the *Sumba* cut away from the open to strike for the cover of the trees which grew along the thin backbone of the highland to the east. And here the flies came down upon them, flies whose bite seemed every bit as bad as a wasp's sting.

"Anoa country," commented van Bleeker. "The black apes like this sort of territory too. Only the island is small for anoa."

"But you are wrong, Captain!" With his rifle Lorens swept back a tangle of grass. "Look here."

Clean and white, polished by the beaks of carrion eaters and the jaws of insects, was a huddle of bones. From their midst the young Netherlander picked up a horned skull.

"Anoa," agreed the captain.

But Kane was more intereted in the hole in that skull. Lorens thrust a finger through it.

"Rifle," he commented. "And recent too. Someone was hunting for the pot and did their butchering on the spot — "

"How long ago, do you think?" the American wanted to know.

"In this climate — who can tell? Perhaps not more than a week."

Fortnight had pushed past them, nosing into the bushes ahead as if he were a hound trying to pick up a scent. Van Bleeker called to him.

"Any sign?"

The big Samoan shook his head. "Not here, Captain. But it would be well to advance cautiously. Shall I try for a trail?"

It was Kane who answered first. "Look here, if this is hunting ground I don't think there will be many trails. As you say, Captain, the island is so small it cannot support much in the way of animal life. Suppose that the cave dwellers, whoever they are, have realized that. Won't they be keeping their hunting to a minimum? And that would mean they would stay pretty much to the other side of the river. I don't think we'll find a path until we get over there."

Kane's deduction must have been the correct one, for, after they left the body of the anoa, they came across no other evidence that anyone had skirted these trees or plowed through the tough grass before them. While they were still some distance from the river they came to a clump of trees whose bright green trunks towered into the sky. And beneath the circle of leaves which topped them almost fity feet above were pods, thick and brownish green.

"Kapok!" Van Bleeker circled the largest of the trees, his head back at an awkward angle as he tried to count the pods. "That's sure proof of cultivation — those aren't native to islands this far north. They've been planted here — "

But he could arouse little interest in kapok. Sam, Kane, and Fortnight were thrusting on toward the river, with Lorens hovering impatiently for the captain to catch up.

"It just occurs to me" — Sam was lying full length behind a bush, peering down into the channel of the stream — "that it might be well for us to avoid the paths after all — remember Burma?"

Kane nipped his lower lip between his teeth. "D'you suppose I could forget it in a hurry? But planting those path traps is a dacoit trick — these natives may not know it — "

"Sharp bamboo is not hard to find hereabouts. Anyway I'd watch where I was putting my feet. Better pass that warning along. Shall we try getting across now?"

While one kept guard on the bank Fortnight and Sam decided between them which was to make the first break. The Samoan won and slipped down the bank to plunge thigh deep through the stream and scramble up the opposite side without waste of time or motion. So one by one they crossed over into the land of the caves.

And there was a trail, wide and firmly packed. The men whose feet had beaten that road had had no reason to be afraid of anything. But the men from the *Sumba* did not follow it. Both the Americans nourished unpleasant memories of the surprises to be found along just such thoroughfares in Burma, and van Bleeker was not ignorant of the man traps which ring in the villages of headhunters in the island world. They were wary of easy trails and kept to the bush.

Which meant swinging bolos again. But, Kane comforted himself, if their coming had not yet been noted by spies, the cave dwellers must be blind, deaf, and idiotic. A little noise couldn't damn them now.

With Fortnight leading they single-filed in the direction of the cliffs. Suddenly the Samoan stopped and gestured the others to look into a clearing.

Regular lines of plants cut the dark soil, a soil clear enough of weeds to testify that this garden was well tended. Van Bleeker identified the find in a harsh whisper, "Camates."

Camates, the sweet potato of the tropics, the staple rough food of the natives from the Philippines south. A camate patch, well kept, and with its potates about ready to harvest, meant a settled community.

"Almost ready to harvest — " Islandwise eyes marked that fact as important, and Kane wondered why.

"Nine months here at least then," went on van Bleeker.

So that was it — nine months of tending meant that the cave dwellers had been here at least that long. But if they numbered among them the survivors of the bomber in the lagoon — why had they not hailed the *Sumba*?

"This garden patch runs east to the cliff base — " pointed out Sam. "Shall we work along it?"

But there was something in the silence of the tree-ringed clearing which made Kane uneasy. Sam and Fortnight slipped away toward the cliff, not waiting for agreement. Van Bleeker appeared to be inclined to shuffle after them, his tail of native seamen with him. But Lorens still lingered. Then the Netherlander stepped out into the soft earth of the bed and studied the ground, remaining there until Kane joined him.

It was easy to see the spoor which had held Lorens' attention. A heel print traced in the soil. Someone, wearing European style shoes, had set his foot there — recently.

"What — " began Kane. But he didn't get his answer from van Norreys.

Did the sharp crack of sound come before the blow on his shoulder whirled him off balance — or after? He groveled into the rich muck of the garden instinctively, even before he felt the stinging burn of the furrow cut into his flesh.

"A sniper!" He attempted to pull the Reising into firing position. But there was no target. Only madly waving fronds showed where the *Sumba*'s men had taken cover.

Spitting mud, Kane raised himself on his elbows and began a careful check of the jungle front. Whoever the sniper was — he must be an old hand at this particular game, though even an amateur could have found excellent cover anywhere around here.

The burn on his shoulder was steadying into an ache. And when he moved his arm molten fire bit deep. But the start he gave when a palm fell against the small of his back made him set his teeth just in time against a real cry of pain.

"Slide back." The order was a half-whisper which was almost a hiss. "Pass me your gun — "

Kane relaxed his hold on the Reising as Lorens' hand

gripped the butt. Slowly he made a worm's progress back to the full cover of the jungle. Once the green veil there closed about him, he turned over and pulled himself up with his back against a tree bole.

The damage, he decided, a moment later, was not much although he was gory enough. Blood was soaking through his shirt, and he could feel it trickling down back and ribs. He was afraid to touch the wound with his earthy hands, nor did he dare to pull the cloth away from that point on his shoulder halfway between arm and neck. If he could avoid infection, there was certainly nothing to play the baby over.

"Dutch! What is it?" Sam wriggled to him just as Lorens backed up, still facing the garden.

Kane spat out more mud. "Just got me a crease. That guy over there must be a rotten shot. Luckily he picked the left shoulder. Any of you fellows have an idea where he's roosting now?"

"That would be hard to say." Van Bleeker came crashing up. "I have told Fortnight to scout. But you, my friend, must return to the *Sumba*. Yes, that I insist upon — as should your own good judgment. In these lands we do not trifle with wounds, even the smallest. It must be treated against infection. Also, we must plan better. As it is, these cave people can hide out and pick us off at their convenience. As I have said from the first, we must discover their back door to win the game — "

Using more precautions now, they retraced their steps and crossed the stream to head for the hook of land where they had first come ashore. Fortnight did not join the retreat. And the fact that they had heard no more shots was no proof that the Samoan had not been ambushed. There were many ways to kill or trap a man in the jungle — without resorting to bullets.

"It's stopped bleeding." Sam had fallen a step or two behind to see the taller man's shoulder.

"I said it was just a scratch, didn't I?" demanded Kane heatedly. "Twist a handkerchief over it and it'll be all right. I'd like to know where Fortnight is — "

"Do not worry about him." Van Bleeker wasn't, that was plain. "He is clever and knows what he is doing. He may bring news which will save us much trouble later."

They passed the bones of the anoa and crossed the last strip of open land. But the boat was not waiting for them. Van Bleeker scuffed impatiently through the sand to the water's edge. He turned to give an order to one of his men just as the scow came into sight, creeping along the shore at a snail's pace although two men in it labored at the oars with an effort which could almost be shared by the watchers on the shore.

One of the rowers was the chief engineer. His face was scarlet to its second roll of chin, and as soon as he saw the captain his mouth began to open and shut as if he were delivering a message which he had not the strength left to shout aloud.

"Where're the other men?" Sam narrowed his eyes against the glare of the sun on the water. "I can only see two."

"There's someone in the bottom of the boat." Lorens shaded his eyes with his hand. "They must have had trouble too — " They had, the sort of trouble which sent van Bleeker a little mad with rage. What touched the *Sumba* and her crew touched him — and in his most sensitive feelings.

"What happened?" His demanding bull roar drowned out the first of Bridger's words. The chief pawed at his dripping face and tried again.

"Sniped us — " he bawled. "Shot Kanaka and Red. Red's hit real bad. But we saw it first! They've got a sub 'round there, Cap'n, a real sub!"

Van Bleeker splashed through the shallows, the rest not far behind him.

"What about Fortnight?" Kane winced as Sam and Lorens boosted him over into the boat. "We can't leave him — "

"He's an eel in the water." The young Netherlander came down beside the American without a jar. "If we can't send back for him, he'll swim out — "

Van Bleeker was down beside the two men in the bottom of the boat. One was very still and limp, but the other moaned, clutching at one arm with his other hand.

"A sub." Sam repeated the word almost unbelievingly. "What kind of a hornets' nest have we blundered into anyway?"

14

ENTER THE MORO NAVY

The main cabin of the *Sumba* was furnace-hot, and the faint corruption of spilled blood tainted what air there was. Felder worked over the unconscious Red, shaving off his crest of coarse flaming hair and capping the injured skull with a thick turban of bandages. Kanaka, Red's fellow in suffering, was sitting up now, grinning a little crookedly, his splinted arm in a sling. Kane buttoned a clean shirt over the patch of cotton and tape which was his battle decoration, intending to escape as soon as possible to the deck where a wandering breeze might settle his sudden squeamishness.

"Now what is this about a submarine?" Van Bleeker stood, hands on hips, in the doorway of the improvised hospital, to challenge Bridger. But the chief was more intent on Felder's first aid than on any report to his captain.

"Oh, there's a sub there right enough. How about it, Felder? Is he — ?"

The second mate straightened to his full height. "With

head wounds one is never sure, you understand. If the bone is not touching the brain — he will wake with the headache, a bad one. But without x-rays — how can one be sure?"

"Move him to my cabin — if he can be moved?" Van Bleeker waited for the second officer's verdict. "Sing can look after him and call us if we are needed. But, Bridger, this submarine now — of what navy was it?"

"German, I think. She wasn't American by th' look o' her rig, nor one o' th' Dutch or English either. I had good sight o' all them durin' th' war. Nor was she like that Jap what shelled th' *Carrie O.* Fact — don't think I've ever seen one jus' like her before. So maybe she's German — "

"Do you mean," Kane broke in, "that there's harborage for a sub on the other side of the island? Then why didn't we see her from the mountain?"

"Maybe 'cause she's under water," returned Bridger calmly. "She's got about six feet o' water over her — only her tower must be awash at low tide. Looks as if someone run her in an' jus' left her there — "

"Which," Sam countered, "may be the truth, at that. Suppose a Nazi sub was caught in these waters during the end-of-the-war confusion. Remember all those stories about high-up Nazis trying to escape to Japan on planes or subs? Well, a sub can't refuel herself. This might have been as far as one could go, having taken a roundabout course to dodge allied ships. It all adds up!"

"Which would put her crew ashore to be our cave dwellers," Lorens mused. "We shall have good reason to go carefully if that is true, Captain. I have come against such hold-out groups before — they call them 'werewolves', and they are utterly vicious. For them there will be no quarter given."

"How long would you say the sub had been there?" Kane asked.

"How can I tell? Maybe weeks, maybe months. Before we had a chance to get a really good look at her they started shootin'. Red got his right away, and when Kanaka went down we had to get out quick. They coulda picked us off like we was ducks in a shootin' gallery."

"Could it have been there as long as the plane in the coral reef?"

Bridger shook his head. "Can't say. Only I don't reckon so."

"Nazis — if they are Nazis — " Lorens was following his own stream of thought. "They will be desperate men — and will fight hard. Only we shall win — "

Sam regarded him curiously. "You're sure of that?"

The Netherlander's lips curled in what was more of a snarl than a smile. "Yes. You see, I have met this breed many times before. And they can always be defeated by the unexpected — because they think in a regular pattern, and if their opponent does not follow the rules, they are lost. When they come up against guerrilla forces, against the Underground, they are on the defensive — and many times they are bewildered. They understand mechanical warfare perfectly and excel at it, because with machines they are at home. They admire and revere the orderly sweep of a Panzer drive. But use against them the gadfly technique, stab and away, confront them with an army which melts into thin air after each attack, an army which will not stand up to a pitched battle, and they lose first their tempers, and then their confidence, and then they are ours."

"The old Red Coat vs. Frontiersman stuff," Kane said. "Well, it won us two wars. And it still works. All right — how can we use it here?"

"Plans must wait until Fortnight reports." Lorens' voice was crisp; there was authority in it. He was on his own ground now. "If our cave dwellers *are* Nazi sub sailors they must have some natives under their control.

To contact them would be a good move — "

"Sure. After some months of life with the gentle Nazi they should be only too glad to help us get rid of them," Sam agreed. "Only, what if the natives are Japs? Don't forget that they know the islands, and that garden and such may be their doing — "

"We must find the back door!" Van Bleeker was back on his favorite theme. "Climb the mountain and hunt for it there — "

"No Jap or Nazi would make an offering to Siva," Kane said thoughtfully. "That seems to indicate that there are some natives here also. Maybe the path down the mountain to the other side is their secret, and the sub men don't know of it. We could scout around and see."

"With a sniper or snipers laying for us?" inquired Sam. "They must have a lookout of their own up there now — they'd want to keep an eye on the *Sumba*. We can't hope to have another undisputed climb. And do any of you fancy doing that bit up the cliff from the old road while some trigger-happy Johnny takes pot shots at you? It won't be any picnic. If we had a plane and could jump — "

Van Bleeker seriously considered that suggestion for a whole moment before he shook his head. "It would take too long to fly a plane here. I shall radio Besi the situation and have the message relayed to your people in Manila. But it will be a long time before they send assistance."

"Now that the war's over the red tape merchants have moved in — sure, we all know that," agreed Sam. "Suits me. We can do this job without the marines. Only we ought to case it first — "

"Case It?" repeated Lorens in puzzlement.

"Look it over, map it out," translated Kane. "I wish Fortnight would turn up."

"I have a man stationed to watch the shore for him," van Bleeker said. "If he signals we'll send a boat for him.

Yes, I, too, would like to hear his report before we move again. Only — I still believe that our solution lies in the mountain."

It was not only the ship's lookout who caught the first sight of the returning Samoan. Lorens, Kane, and Sam busied at arms inspection on deck all saw the tall man break out of the jungle cover and trot down the scrap of beach. He hesitated at the water's edge for only a moment, then before the ship's boat could cast off for him, he waded into the sea, holding his rifle over his head.

When the boat picked him up and headed back for the *Sumba*, most of her officers, all of her passengers and as many of her crew as could find excuse, were waiting on deck for him to come overside. Almost before his feet touched deck planking he called out to the captain, "Schooner coming in, sir — straight for the reef break — she seems to know the course."

With one vicious spat of order van Bleeker sent a seaman up to the lookout's post.

"Sure it's a schooner and not a prau?" asked Sam.

Fortnight paid no attention to the interruption.

"I give her half an hour, maybe a little more. She's a trader, well equipped and sailing under engine. There's something familiar about her too — "

"How did you sight her?"

"From up there." Fortnight jerked his head toward the mountain in answer to Kane's question. "I was on my way back when I saw her first."

"Then there is a way over the mountain from the other side!"

The Samoan half smiled. "Yes. But one I would not care to use again. It is both known and guarded."

"You say that the schooner's familiar," van Bleeker cut in. "Can't you remember where you've seen her before?"

Fortnight shrugged. "I have been cruising these islands for years and have seen many ships. But I think that it is not long since I saw her last."

The lookout shouted, his deep-throated cry bringing him all their attention. He repeated his information, and van Bleeker gave a visible start.

"So that is the way of it!"

"What's the matter?" Kane voiced their common question.

"She is the *Drinker of the Wind*, old Hakroun's flagship and personal yacht. And she's heading straight for here."

"So the old Moro is going to take a hand in the business?" asked Sam. "That's all we need to complete this party — three parties of us taking pot shots at each other and a naval engagement in the lagoon!"

"How do you know that Abdul is not backing the cave force?"

"I don't. But it is more likely that that diver we picked up was one of Hakroun's men. And did he look as if he had the good will of anyone? It's my reasoning that the old boy has come to start a private war of his own." Sam hesitated, then stopped, because he discovered that he had the full attention of his audience. Even van Bleeker was listening to every word.

"You may be very right," the captain observed. "We shall prepare for action, but then we shall wait for Hakroun to give it to us. For his objective may be ours also, and he is an old hand at such games — an ally not to be despised."

"If you win Hakroun as an ally," Lorens pointed out, "then you have won your war. I do not think he is coming here with less than a full expeditionary force. If all the tales they tell of him are true, he may even produce a tank or a bomber. He has his methods of finding just what he needs and wants."

The *Drinker of the Wind* seemed to lose a little of her

confidence when she sighted the *Sumba*. It was Sam's contention that she backed, as might a startled cat when rounding a corner to confront a dog. The Moro schooner made no attempt to enter the lagoon. Instead a boat was lowered, and several well-armed natives tumbled down into it. They took to oars with a will and set a course for the reef break, riding in on the roll of the waves with the ease of voyagers who had performed that trick successfully many times before.

Once inside the reef they made for the *Sumba*, hailing her as soon as they came within voice range.

"Come aboard!" was van Bleeker's counter.

Kane recognized in the first man to board the second son of Abdul Hakroun. The Moro gazed around him at crew, ship, and passengers with polite interest, but beyond the greeting demanded by island ceremony, he did not speak until the captain invited him into the cabin.

"You have been here long?" Kuran waved aside the proffered glass of refreshment.

"Long enough — " the captain parried.

"Long enough for trouble to find you?" Kuran's brown eyes rested for a moment on the bandage, plainly outlined beneath Kane's thin shirt. "You discovered thorns in the jungle?"

"Were *you* expecting to find thorns there?" Lorens asked. "Perhaps they were planted by — "

The Moro laughed, a sharp bark of sound which had a sting in it. "My honored father is much interested in thorns and islands. Since the infirmities of age bind him to the cabin of the *Drinker*, he begs your indulgence and asks that you visit him, so that we may discuss thorns — and other things — at leisure."

"Has he been thorn-pricked also?" Lorens asked.

But van Bleeker was annoyed. "The lagoon is wide enough for both the *Sumba* and the schooner. Why don't you bring her in?"

Sword In Sheath

For a long moment Kuran's silent will battled the stubbornness of the Dutchman. Then the Moro arose with a little inclination of his head.

"I will make your suggestion to my honored father. It will be for him to then decide."

Van Bleeker snorted as he watched the boat draw away from the *Sumba* and head for the schooner.

"Wanted to get us on his home ground, did he? Well, two can play at any game that old devil thinks up. Now, Fortnight, tell us quickly what you saw ashore. If we have information Hakroun wants, we shall have the best of any bargain he tries to make. Who are these cave men and what are they doing here?"

"Some are white men or natives dressed as whites and some Japanese. There are natives, too, but not many. They live in the five caves highest in the cliff, and the approach to each is well defined. Nothing but a real expeditionary force can pull them out of there."

"The map — " Van Bleeker waved them back to the cabin and brought out the map Lorens had sketched. "Show us on here — "

"There, there, and there." Fortnight pointed out the fortifed caves. "And here is the path up the mountain, easy to climb. It ends here in the crater behind the large spur of rock to the west of the temple entrance. But I was followed up there, and they will be waiting now for anyone who tries to use it."

"Are the white men Nazis?" asked Lorens.

"I cannot be sure of anything save that maybe they are white. There are only a few of them — maybe five or six — and they seem to stay together in this topmost cave. I do not think that they are entirely happy with their Japanese companions. One of them tried to urge on the Japs to follow me, but he had little success. Maybe because I had already made two very lucky shots." The Samoan grinned happily.

"Where there is one trail there may be another," the captain mused. "I say we should try the mountain again. It is easy enough for a sniper to work in the jungle — but there is cover for us on the mountain."

"It comes back," Kane pointed out wearily, "to the old problem of how we are going to get into the crater without being ambushed. That one stretch of trail where the climb is so tough cannot be done without cover — and there's none of that. Unless we can bypass that, such a climb would be suicide."

"Captain, the schooner is coming in," Felder reported quietly.

They were all on deck to watch the *Drinker of the Wind* come into position smartly, and across the water the roar of her anchor chain paying out came to their ears.

There was a flurry of activity on the schooner's deck, a coming and going of long-robed personages. Suddenly the Dutch captain sucked in his breath sharply and turned to shout down the deck.

"You — Karma and Yee — rig a bosun's chair and make it quick — to starboard!"

"It's the old devil himself." The captain turned back to his passengers. "Abdul's coming to call!"

"What!" Lorens pushed against the rail.

A ship's boat crept out from the schooner. She was loaded, even overloaded, with a motley crew of natives, all of whom seemed to be armed with the very latest in rifles or sub-machine guns. Gun smuggling, Kane thought to himself, must be a very good business hereabout. Surely Hakroun had never gained all those by any legitimate means.

As the boat nosed against the *Sumba*'s side the mass of retainers and henchmen swarmed up. Four of them elbowed away the seamen of the Dutch ship and took over the lowering of the bosun's chair for the convenience of their leader. And so quick were they about the business that van Bleeker and the others had just time to reach the lower deck as the found green dome of their unbidden guest's turban arose above the rail.

The sonorous phrases of greeting rolled through the air and van Bleeker ordered that cushions be spred in the shade beneath an awning strip. So there they settled down cross-legged, Abdul, with his fighting men at his back and van Bleeker, Lorens, the two Americans and the ever silent mate, across from them. Those members of the *Sumba*'s crew who could find or invent a reason began to drift on deck and squat down within listening distance. Kane glanced around. The meeting had taken on the air of a peace conference between rival powers. Which was just what it was in truth.

For once Abdul Hakroun came to the point swiftly and cleanly — a kris cutting butter.

"You have had trouble with them." Native fashion he pointed to the island with his chin.

"Some." Van Bleeker was wary. "We were fired upon when we tried to explore."

"You are lucky that it was no worse." The old Moro's fingers were in his beard. "Those are desperate men who hide yonder. They are without hope and when Allah — may His Name be ever exalted — takes from a man his hope there is nothing left. My countrymen run 'amok' as you say of them. These men do that now — their hands are raised against the whole world. They are as mad dogs and must be put to the sword — "

"How do you know so much about them?" the captain asked.

The hand in the fringe of beard was still, but the hooded eyes did not blink.

"I had a trading post here, and these wild beasts destroyed it. When word of that disaster was brought to me I came — to measure justice. If the cloak of my protection covers a man, then I exact vengence for him.

There has been blood shed here — blood of those of my household. I come to uphold my honor!"

"And what do you want of us?"

Both ivory hands came out of the beard. "Blood of your men has been shed also. We have a common cause. Shall we not wield then a common sword? This cancer has become a stench through the islands; it is time to burn it out!"

15

VOICE FROM THE NIGHT

W hen van Bleeker made no immediate answer to the amazing proposition of Abdul Hakroun, the old man spoke again, a sort of dry amusement coloring his rich voice.

"I am now a wizard of gifts," he announced with mocking solemnity, "for I can read your present thoughts, Captain. They are these — Why does this Hakroun wish to make terms with me? What lies hidden on this island which he is so determined to gain that he must treat with the men of the *Sumba* to get it?

"And there you have your answer, Tuan Captain. There is a treasure here for the finding. Oh, it is not the pearl beds which you must already have located, being neither stupid men nor those unfortunates from whom Allah, in His Infinite Wisdom, removed the power of sight.

"Some weeks ago a Japanese, calling himself a trader, came to Manado in quest of passage north to his own land. During some converse with him an agent of mine discovered that he was a messenger from this very island. It was from his hands that my agent had that Nararatna which you, Tuan van Norreys, were so very loath to buy. May I be permitted to ask why — it was a famous bargain?"

Those bright eyes shifted to Lorens, and the young Netherlander half smiled.

"It was too great a bargain — "

Abdul Hakroun gave a clicking sound of annoyance. "I am indeed growing old when the suckling babes of the trade suspect my intentions. But that Nararatna came from here, of that I have sufficient proof. And where one wonder is found, a keen-nosed man may perhaps sniff out another. So we have pearls and a treasure. Is that not lure enough to pull any man hither?"

"Pearls, treasure *and* a trading post," van Bleeker reminded him.

"A looted trading post." The correction was quick. "Yes, there is also the matter of vengence and the settling of scores with the rabble hiding here. They are of that sort for which you Americans and Dutch have been hunting the world over during the past few years, Nazis and Japanese turned pirates — for that is just what they have become. Here is the source, the home port, of those two pirate praus which have been ranging the southern waters. It is the task set us by Allah to cleanse this place with fire and sword. I had thought to do it alone with my own men, but, since you have found your way here, it is cearly the will of Allah that part of the battle be yours. Also" — the laughter in the old voice bubbled very near the surface — "you are strong men, well armed with the latest weapons. This being so, who am I to stand against the wishes of the Devisor of Destinies? Shall we be allies?"

"Allies or friends?" Lorens brought the challenge into

the open. "There are many allies who unite only for one stroke against a common enemy and then are at each other's throats again when that fight is over. We have no liking for that — "

Hakroun considered before he answered. "Let it be as friends. I perceive that there is a reason in this, that from the first it was meant to happen so. Join me as friends!"

The green-turbaned head was proundly high, the eyes shone as they flicked from face to face of the men facing him. Lord, Kane thought, he's it — the big man! When he gives an order it's obeyed without question! He and Iron-jaw — wouldn't they make a perfect team now? Why — I like the guy!

"Agreed." Van Bleeker's hand went out to engulf the frail claws the other advanced.

"Now." There was no hint of triumph in Hakroun's attitude. He was the businessman getting down to serious work. "Let us plan. We must move before the two praus now cruising return — "

"Praus, you say?"

"Yes. They attack only the smaller native vessels, those which they know can be taken. I have lost ten such within the past six months — and I am not the only one who has suffered. But with both those ships at sea the force they have here must be a small one. We can smoke them out — "

"What about the sub?" Kane ventured his first question. "If they can use her we'll have trouble."

"Sub?" The old Moro looked to van Bleeker for enlightenment, and the captain of the *Sumba* told of Bridger's find.

"I think," he concluded, "that they must be out of fuel. Certainly they wouldn't take to praus if they could use it — "

"So-o — " The word was a hiss as Hakroun spoke it. "That is where they obtained the deck gun they carry on the prau which attacked the Red Fish! Where is this sunken ship?"

He made a little gesture, and his son pulled from his sleeve a rolled chart which, when spread out on the flat space of deck planking before Hakroun, proved to be a surprisingly accurate map of the island and surrounding waters. Lorens compared it to the sketch map and pointed out their own observations.

Hakroun had the added advantage of knowing the western side of the island, the cave land. For it had been on a northern finger of that territory that his destroyed trading post had stood. It had not been a real trading post but more of a headquarters for those working the pearling beds.

As far as the Moro trader knew, the handful of timid natives whom his men had found on the island were without any products to trade, and Hakroun's men had not been able to establish any real contact with them in the few weeks which had elapsed between the first settlement of pearl divers and the coming of a strong party of Japanese holdout troops fleeing from the wrath in the lower islands. A night of sharp fighting had settled the argument as to the ownership of the island, and the survivors of Hakroun's forces had fled.

"It was only by chance that my men ever found this land in the first place," Abdul stated frankly. "It is not on any map these old eyes have ever seen. I do not think that even the Japanese, island wise as they made themselves in the past few years, knew it before they came. And of this city or temple in the mountain — of that I know nothing at all — though the Nararatna pointed to the probability of such a place. The natives are but a handful. They have been here a long, long time, and now they die out, after the manner of ancient peoples cut off from the world. They were very shy and would not approach my men. At times we left some trade goods on the rocks for them — it was best to have their good will, you understand. But they did not come for it while any man watched. My people saw them only as shadows. Why should we hunt them down? We have no use for the island; it was the pearls which drew us first, and those are in the sea. So we troubled them not. Doubtless the Japanese have long since put an end to them, as they did with other simple peoples.

"As for your bomber, and those who salvaged her, of that I have no knowledge either. My men saw no Europeans here before they were driven away. Perhaps that was the work of these pirates also."

"You'd think," Kane said suddenly, "that if these fellows had praus and could get away, they'd go, strike out for the mainland. They could land in Siam or the Malay states or even Java — things have been so disorganized down there since the war that they could easily hide out and never be found."

"Why should they?" countered Lorens. "They are the conquered and know that their world has been swept away. Here they have a measure of security and can keep alive the legend of the invincible supermen. If they had not had the ill luck to enounter your men" — he nodded courteously to Hakroun — "they might have remained here — maybe for years — without being hunted down."

"That is the truth," agreed the Moro, "but to it add another rumor which has been carried to these old ears. There are those in the islands for whom the struggle for power has just begun, who are being supported from afar. They are quick to seize upon opportunity and to enlist masterless men. Such a colony as this one is a tool ready to their ultimate purpose. A man's coat and allegiance are easily changed when his belly is empty, his leaders dead, and naught but death before him. A handful of supplies, shadowy encouragement, and the hope of a better future will bring even these wolves to heel — "

"The same old story," muttered Sam. "Here we go again — "

"If they are practicing pirates," Kane pointed out, "there probably *is* a treasure hoard here."

Hakroun was tracing the coast line on the map and listening to van Bleeker's arguments about the desirability of discovering a back door into the cave territory. When the Dutch captain had finished the Moro clapped his hands and called, "Mahaud!"

Out of the company of armed-to-the-teeth warriors who lounged behind him crawled an odd little person, a scarlet rag serving him for a turban and another of bright yellow for a loin cloth. He nursed in his crooked arm, against the misshapen barrel of his chest, a bolo almost as long as his stunted body.

"Could Mahuad take this path of the apes which you have spoke of?" Abdul asked Kane.

The dwarfish figure was certainly not much taller than the black apes who had found and made their own the side entrance to the temple.

"I think so," the American replied. "But he would have to reach the crater before he tried it, and there are several places along the way where they could easily ambush him. The climb is a difficult one."

"It is as Allah wills," was Hakroun's pious rejoinder. "I shall send a man ashore — one who was here before and knows the island. We shall learn more of their defenses —   "

So ended the conference aboard the *Sumba*, without really deciding anything, Sam pointed out — the usual result when the big brass gets together.

"Anyway our mission," the Nisei concluded, "is to find out about that bomber. Let's don't get drawn into a private war and forget all about it. Abdul is fighting for that pearl bed and, I'll bet, for any loot these Nazis and

Japs have managed to snaffle and pile up here. Van Bleeker can't lose out either. If he backs up Abdul and they win, the old boy will have to cut him in on both deals. That goes for your friend van Norreys too. But us, we won't be in on that. The bomber's our job. Don't forget that we bought that dollar from a Jap — "

"I'm not forgetting it, nor the bomber either. Only you heard what Hakroun said. His men were here months ago and saw no white men — before the killers came."

"And what'll you wager that they didn't look very hard? They didn't have much contact with the natives. And suppose our fellows were hurt, maybe out of their heads or down with malaria. They might not even have known about Hakroun's men being here. I've a hunch that we've come to the right place — "

"All right, all right!" Kane put his hand on the cabin latch. "In the meantime I'm going to have me a nap. I'm the wounded hero — remember?"

But Sam trailed along into the cabin and fidgeted around while Kane spread himself across the lower bunk. The Nisei was examining the smooth expanse of sheet and pillow of his own sleeping place when Kane glanced up.

"Lose something?"

"Where's that darn cat? First time since we sailed that she hasn't been enjoying herself at our expense — you'd think she was paying for this cabin."

The cat!

"Good lord!" Kane lifted his head from the pillow with a snap. "Bridger will have my hide for sure."

Sam regarded him with interest. "What did you do — pitch her overboard?"

"No. But she went on our little exploring party this morning. Crawled over me so she could hit the beach before we did. And I don't think I've seen her since."

"She certainly wasn't in the boat that brought us

back," said Sam. "Seems to me that there is a story about rats deserting a sinking ship — Wonder if it holds good for cats too. What do you suppose she went ashore for?"

"Hunting, I guess. D'you think I ought to find Bridger and confess?"

"Confess what? You didn't invite her to go along, did you? It was her own idea. Maybe she likes the cave dwellers better. Judging by what I've seen of her she is well able to take care of herself."

Sam gathered up some papers and a book and went out, leaving his companion to the warm silence of the cabin. And after a while Kane did sleep. He woke at last, a fiery ball of pain in his shoulder where he had rolled upon the furrowed cut. It was dusky both within the cabin and outside on deck. And now there was a breeze from off island which felt good on his head and shoulders when he got on his feet. He snapped on the light, and, as if that was a signal, the Malay steward appeared, genii-wise.

"Mijnheer wishes supper?"

"Where is everybody?" Kane was suddenly aware of the unusual silence. Not that the *Sumba* was ever a factory of noise, but now there was not even the chatter of a seaman, the contented hum of van Bleeker at his work.

"A messenger came from the other ship, mijnheer. Capt. van Bleeker and the other Tuans speedily departed there."

"How long ago?" Kane was outraged. Sam should have known better than to leave him behind.

"An hour, maybe more, mijnheer."

Kane's fingers fumbled as he fastened on the belt of his automatic. If they were going to storm ashore tonight and Sam had deliberately left him out of it — ! He might be nicked in the shoulder, but he was a long way removed from the invalid list — as Sam would discover.

The steward still hovered behind him.

"Well?" Kane barked.

"If the mijnheer pleases — has he seen the cat? She has not come to the galley for her food?"

The cat!

"She went ashore this morning in the boat. I don't think she came back."

"But, mijnheer, why should she do that? She has never before — "

"Don't ask me. How long did you say Capt. van Bleeker and the other Tuans have been gone?"

"An hour, maybe a little more. There came someone from the other ship — "

"As you said before. Are they planning to go ashore?"

"That I do not know, mijnheer."

"Well, who does? How can I get over there?"

The rising moon made a molten silver floor of the lagoon water but not one substantial enough to walk across.

"Mijnheer T'ang is on deck — "

Kane was already on his way to hunt down the mate of the *Sumba*. He must catch up with Sam and the rest before they really started something. The clatter of his steps sounded unnaturally loud, even in his own ears, as he hurried along, staring at each shadow in his search for T'ang.

He found the mate near the somewhat blunt bow of the freighter. The first officer's cigarette was a tiny dot of light in the dark as he lounged against the rail, his attention all for the dark bulk of the island. Kane glanced landward too. The hump of the mountain was a misshapen lump of black with the silver water lapping hungrily at its foot. But it might have been a dead land on another planet. If the cave dwellers had lights they did not use them or else such illumination could only be seen from the west.

T'ang turned. He was tall even for a half-caste, taller than the American. His beardless face was smooth, unreadable. But he stood in an attitude of polite inquiry, waiting for Kane to speak first.

"Can you set me aboard the schooner?"

"If you wish it, mijnheer. Now?"

"I suppose so. Are they going to try something to-night?"

"I think not, mijnheer. To attack in the darkness, when we know so little of the land — that would be only foolishness. No, they plan for tomorrow. But I will give orders for the boat to be lowered for you. A few minutes only will it take."

He didn't turn away from the rail, however. Instead he hunched forward suddenly in one supple movement, the whole length of his body outlining the effort he was making to see through the night. And Kane crowded up beside him.

"What is it?"

"There is a swimmer in the water. See, from the beach there, someone is swimming toward the *Sumba!*"

For a long time the American saw nothing, then a break in the silver surface of the water showed so clearly he wondered at his own blindness. He caught the flash of what could only be a swimmer's arms.

"Hakroun sent a man ashore — "

"He returned before their council. This is not one of ours."

There was something bright in T'ang's right hand. He was raising an automatic — but the American moved first.

"Don't shoot! If there's only one, let's get him. He'll have information."

"To render a serpent harmless, cut off his head."

"All right, but do your head cutting after I have had a chance to ask a few questions. Yes, he's coming up about here. Let's go and be a reception committee."

"Where?" T'ang sounded amused. "The ladder has been taken up. Having suspicions of just such visits I ordered it hauled up after the captain's party left — "

"Can't we put it down again? We may not have another chance like this. Do something, won't you?" But Kane's impatience did not add any speed to the mate's deliberate pace.

"There is time," he reproved the American. "And we can handle the ladder, yes."

With the American's help the ladder was put in place, then they waited above, keeping to the shadows where the moon could not finger them out.

"He is no native," T'ang whispered. "and he is not a good swimmer either. He is beginning to tire."

Kane could see little difference in the progress of those arms and the body which they must be propelling, but then T'ang was more islandwise than he.

The swimmer was beside the *Sumba*, and one hand clawed upward to hook on the ladder. But he made no move to drag himself out of the water, only held to the wood and rope as if that alone had been the goal for which he had battled.

T'ang venturned out of the shadow and peered down. "He is done."

But the words, or perhaps just the sound of a voice, injected a last bit of energy into that limp body below.

"For God's sake — give me a hand! Help!"

Kane slipped over the rail, his feet finding the rungs of the ladder. He went down as quickly as he could in spite of his burning shoulder, down to that voice out of the night — the voice which had called out in very good English!

16

THE ROAD OF THE GODS

Between them, the mate and Kane got the swimmer to the deck, then T'ang, refusing help, carried the limp body into the wardroom, where, for the first time, they were able to see their prize in the full glare of the cabin lights.

He lay quiet, an amazing amount of water oozing out of his few rags of clothing and his matted hair and beard. The skin, stretched tightly over his too-apparent bones, was tanned brown, but it had once been white, as white as Kane's own. This man was no island native.

But it was just as plain that he had been having a hard time. There were purple bruises on his face, and when T'ang brought towels and they began to rub him down, numerous cuts and scrapes were only too evident. Together his rescuers worked over him until at last he opened his eyes.

"Hello — ?" That voice might be weak, but it was steady enough, and there was the light of reason in the eyes above the tangle of neglected beard.

"Hello," Kane returned cheerfully. "How do you feel?"

Teeth showed in a wide grin. "Just tops, brother, after hearing you. When did the marines arrive?"

"Were you expecting them?"

"Well, a guy can always hope. Seriously, though, what outfit is this, buddy?"

"We're sort of a mixed dish — Dutch, American, and Moro. And you?"

"Technical Sergeant Tucker Watson, United States Army Air Force. You took long enough getting here, fella. When did you pick up our signals?"

"Your signals?" Kane's astonishment was equaled by the other's surprise at his reaction.

"Didn't you come because you heard Pete's calls?"

"Who's Pete? No, we just drifted in here, mostly by blind luck. Do you mean that there is a bunch of you fellows ashore here — along with the pirates?"

"There were several of us," corrected Watson. "They got Pete a few weeks back, and that left just me. If it hadn't been for old Toothless hiding me out in the mountain, they'd have added me to their bag. We took a chance trying to make the radio work — that's how they caught Pete. He'd been fussing with it ever since we pulled it out of the drink, thought he could patch it up. But I guess it wasn't much good — "

"How long have you been here?"

"Dunno. A guy sort of loses track of time. We had a calendar we did a lot of guessing on. Say — is the war over?"

Kane nodded. "Little more than a year since the Japs surrendered."

"What did we do to them — blow them off the map?"

"Just about. We let go with an atom bomb."

"Atom bomb!"

"Yeah, we used it twice. Then they gave up. Germany

had folded before that."

"We kind of suspected that — after the Nazis got here. Boy, they were plenty burned up and scared. The Jap leader, Sukimato, tried to stand up to them at first, but he wasn't tough enough. It took Red Turban to pull the right sort of bluff. Now they all play second fiddle — and half the time they're so busy watching each other they forget all about us — "

"Red Turban?"

"Uh-huh. He's top guy here now. Pete said he was either a European gone native — or else a native who lived in Europe a long time. But when he gives orders — do they step! He isn't here all the time, though — goes out with their raiding praus. We sure keep out of sight when he's around."

"Who're we?"

"Well, in the beginning there were Dan, Pete and me. Only Dan pegged out with the fever — we've all had it bad. Then Pete said we'd better take cover with Tooth-less' gang, they know the island's insides — the whole mountain is hollow with passages. We went in with them when the first gang of Japs arrived. That is, we thought they were Japs — but now I'm beginning to wonder. They were peaceful cusses, kept to their own place down on the point and actually left out some trade goods for Toothless' folks. Then this other crowd under Sukimato breezed in, and there was a grand blow-up. Sukimato's men won out. So we took to the mountain with Toothless — while Pete tinkered with the radio. He wanted to broadcast the whole business with the hope that some-one could pick up the message. I was laid up with a bad foot, cut it on coral and had a devil of a time getting over the infection. So one day Pete went out with one of the native kids, and the Japs got them both. After that I just stayed on in the mountain with the rest of the islanders.

"Then we heard about this ship, and I was sure Pete

Sword In Sheath   **191**

had done it after all — got the message through, I mean. I was doubly sure after the cat came — "

"The cat?"

"Yeah. She crawled into our hideout this morning, made herself right at home. I kind of thought she came from a ship with white officers 'cause she was friendly with me from the start. So tonight I took a chance and swam out."

"Do you know a way across the mountain — one the Japs haven't found?"

"Sure. They aren't so smart, and old Toothless knows this place through and through. The Nazi crowd moved into some of the caves, but they haven't even found all of them. If we'd had anything but those old rusty swords and spears Toothless nurses, we could have cleaned 'em out ourselves. But of course we'd have to do it while most of them were at sea — like right now."

"Boy, oh, boy!" Kane grinned down at Watson. "Are you a find! Did you hear that, T'ang? This tuan" — he slipped into Coast Malay — "knows of a secret way across the mountain. He is of my nation and has been hiding from the pirates."

The mate nodded. "Shall I send for Capt. van Bleeker? He should know of this."

"Where's the big guy going?" Watson watched T'ang out of the cabin.

"Most of our gang is over on Hakroun's schooner holding a gabfest about how we're going to cross the mountain without being shot up in some ambush. T'ang's going to send for them. Now, how about some nourishment — ?"

"When you say that, fella," commented the skeleton on the lounge, "you'd better mean it! I've been dipping into caveman messes so long I wouldn't know how to use a fork — "

"Then maybe soup'd go down better. We'll try that

first."

So when the party from the schooner stormed into the cabin some time later it was to find Kane feeding Watson, spoon by steaming spoon. For the gunner, having burned out his strength in that last desperate swim, was unable to raise his wasted hands to his mouth.

"Take it easy," Kane growled at the newcomers, "he's about done in."

But that they had already seen for themselves, edging back from the lounge to allow the American room in his self-appointed task.

"How's that?" he asked as the spoon scraped the bottom of an empty bowl.

"Swell, just swell. Haven't got a real smoke on you, have you?"

It was Lorens who produced the cigarette, put it between the thin lips, and lighted it, almost all in one swift movement. After Watson had drawn deep the Netherlander withdrew it for an instant while the rescued man puffed out the fragrant smoke. Then Watson sighed.

"Swell — just swell," he repeated drowsily.

Lorens was feeling for the pulse in a bony wrist. Then he nodded almost imperceptibly at Kane.

"Suppose you take a nap." The American caught the message and acted upon it. "We can do the rest of our gabbing later — we have all the time in the world now — "

"Sure — all the time in the world — " The eyelids closed, and Watson was in the heavy sleep of exhaustion.

Kane pulled the cotton blanket up over the bruised shoulders and followed the rest out of the cabin.

The sun was already climbing when they gathered there again. Outside the voices of the men, overhauling fighting equipment under the watchful eye of T'ang, made a steady murmur. But within Watson's hesitating words were the only sounds to break the silence of the wardroom.

"Past the outcrop and then straight up and in. You can't see it at first — not until you are almost on it — "

"Go into the small cave." Van Bleeker repeated earlier instructions. "And then climb up — "

"Yes. You may find Toothless' man there — if he isn't too scared. Most of them won't venture in that far — they're afraid of ghosts — it's all connected up with some old chief or king who cursed the place. They think that he engineered the earthquake which killed off most of the people here in the old days. And that climb is no cinch. It's a darn sight easier to come down than go up. Take it slow and easy."

"We come then to the passage which will bring us to the quarters of this chief, and he will provide a guide for the rest of the way?"

"That's right. Toothless doesn't like the Japs one little bit. All he wants is to be let alone. He'll help you 'cause I promised him that you just wanted to run the Japs off. I don't know why you showed up here anyway" — Watson's face, shorn of its mat of beard, was boyish, but there was an odd sort of authority in the way he faced them now — "only I promised Toothless that my kind of American wasn't out to grab all he could get."

Kane shifted uncomfortably. Sam seemed uninterested in the ethics of the case, but the American saw Lorens' grimace of distaste. It was the Netherlander who, after looking to van Bleeker, turned to Kuran who represented his formidable father at the conference and asked, "Does such a promise hold with you?"

"We came for pearls — and for vengeance on the Japanese. We have no need for land. Nor do we wish ill to the men who dwell here rightfully. It is the word of Hakroun that they are not to be troubled."

Van Bleeker was no man for heroic speeches, but his answer was to the point. "I'm a trader. I took a beating in the war. All I have left is the *Sumba* and a stake to give me one more try at the islands. A wise trader does not make trouble for himself. And your island is no good to me. I'd rather have the good will of this chief — "

Watson slipped down against the bolster which propped him up.

"Okay. I'm betting on your meaning that, all of you. Toothless is a right guy, kind of simple and straight-forward. He thought a lot of Pete. 'Course Pete was smart, he'd been to college, was some sort of an engineer before the war. You ought to see the water pipe he rigged up so we'd get water in the caves after the Japs moved in — a slick job! Toothless thought Pete was a big chief too, used to consult him about running things. Say, Sukimato might still have the stuff he took off Pete. I'd like to have it back if you find it. Want to send it home to his folks — "

"I'll get it for you." Sam's promise was confident. He turned to van Bleeker. "When do we start?"

"If they are the men we believe them to be they will have a watch on us now — perhaps from the crater. Therefore we cannot move openly — I say wait until sundown."

Lorens and Kane nodded in agreement, and a second later Kuran gave his approval, but Sam was not con-vinced.

"The longer we let them alone the more time they'll have to cook up something good to meet us with," he warned. "And, if they don't know about this back door in the mountain, what can they do once we're inside? I say move now and be quick about it."

Watson agreed with Sam.

"Toothless will have a hard time holding his men long. They don't like the cave passages on this side at all. And we are sure that the Japs don't know this way. All any scout could see would be you walking into the jungle. He'd wait awhile for you to come out again, not knowing just where you would appear, and that should keep him busy long enough for you all to get into the cave. They will be expecting you to move against them sooner or later anyway — "

"Well?" van Bleeker challenged the rest of them. "What do you say?"

"I say try it now!" That was Sam.

"Guess I'll go along with that." Kane came in a moment later. "What Watson says sounds like sense."

"Go now." Lorens added his voice.

"My men are ready to move," promised the Moro.

"Very well," van Bleeker gave in. "We shall go now. I make every man responsible for his own arms and do not forget your torches — "

Without Watson's patient insistence about keeping their eyes open they might have missed the back door to the mountain. As he had said, it could not be sighted even a few feet away. But they were welcomed by a waiting sentry, a sentry who looped herself lovingly around Kane's ankles and almost tripped him up.

"It's that fool cat!"

"Sure. Didn't Watson say she'd been roosting with him." Sam looked down at the sleek form. "Look out — there she goes — "

Go the *Sumba*'s cat did, into a narrow slit, with the party from her ship and the Moros right behind her. The fault in the rock through which they struggled was so narrow that at times it was necessary to turn sidewise and scrape through. The big Samoan and the tall Kane fared the worst at these spots, and the American wondered if he would have any skin left across shoulders and hips when this little trip was over.

He began to envy the cat who had four feet and no baggage to encumber her in the scramble over the uneven floor of the passage. The light of their electric torches, strong as it was, could not show all the pitfalls, and someone was continually stumbling.

"No wonder Watson looked as if he had just gone ten rounds with a champion," commented Kane. "It's the worst footing I have ever seen. This beats even the New Guinea mud trails!"

"Shut up and get on with it!" snapped Sam from behind. "We haven't all day before us — "

After a particularly nasty climb they pulled themselves into the round mouth of another cave, one of such size that their torches only made a circle of light where they stood. The ring of their boots on the stone echoed loudly, and a formation of bats began dive-bombing their position. The cat was thrown into a frenzy and leaped wildly into the air in pursuit, yowling in fury when she missed.

"Well, where do we go from here?" asked Sam. "Isn't this where the guide was supposed to show up?"

The Moro leader pointed to the right. "There is one who hides there," he stated matter-of-factly.

Jungle wise as they were, none of them could see what Kuran had noted. Van Bleeker moved toward the wall.

"Can you speak with him?" he asked softly of the Moro.

The man shrugged. "I can try." He lapsed into a slurred speech of which Kane could not understand a word.

They waited in silence, then the Moro called again. This time something scuttled away, back into the thick darkness. Kuran sped forward in chase, his men at his back. The party from the *Sumba*, taken by surprise, were slower starters, but they made up for it with a burst of speed which brought them up to jostle the Moros.

"He is afraid of us," the tall Moro leader explained. "But even so he leads us."

"Sure we aren't following a Jap?" demanded Kane.

"No," Fortnight's deep voice boomed out, to be taken up and repeated weirdly by the walls, "it is no Japanese we follow."

They were in a passage now, but this one was relatively smooth under foot. Kane flashed his light at the nearest wall. He had been right in his surmise — the marks of the tools which had been used to break off the rougher projections were still plain to see. At some time and for some reason this had been a thoroughfare for the men of the mountain.

The passage sloped upward gently, in fact they had been climbing ever since they had entered the mountain. Kane tried to figure out whether they were close to the crater, but it was impossible to judge distances when underground.

But it was not into the crater cup that they plunged at the end of the passage. Instead they found themselves on a wide ledge overhanging another cave of large dimensions. The smoky flare of a large fire made a splotch of raw color which lighted up the fantastic scene on the cave floor below.

"Good lord!" gasped Sam. "Arabian nights!"

"It's incredible!" Lorens echoed him.

There were men below, men with steel in their hands and mad contrasts of color in the rags of clothing they wore. Several were capped with helmets from which hung veils of fine chain mail to guard neck and throat. And two carried small round shields on their left forearms.

"Spears — and swords!" Lorens edged to the lip of the ledge. "But it is utterly fantastic!"

There was a shout of warning as someone below sighted them, and the whole unbelievable throng faded into the dark mouths of several passages.

"Now what?" asked Kane. "Do we go below and risk a spear through the gizzard before we have a chance to negotiate properly?"

"Wait!" Lorens still held his point of vantage. "Here

comes someone now. And look at the white flag!"

One of the iron-capped warriors crept out, his two hands before him gripping a spear from the shaft of which drooped a rag which had once perhaps been white. As he came around the fire he turned not toward the center of the ledge where they now stood but toward the far end.

"That must be the way down." Kane made his way cautiously along and was not surprised to find a flight of shallow steps hewn from the rock.

The cave dweller was waiting at their foot, his pathetic flag of truce very much in evidence. Kane, Lorens, and the Moro captain started down.

"Okay," Sam called. "I'll keep him covered. Let him make a wrong move and he gets it right through that tin hat of his!"

But the caveman made no move. And as they came closer Kane saw that he was a very old man, in spite of his erect carriage. The thin beard along his jaw was as white as the eyebrows above the sunken pits of his dark eyes. His mouth was shrunken and puckered, and when he opened it to speak the American saw that his teeth were missing. This must be "Toothless", the chieftain who had Watson's regard and trust. But Kane could make nothing of the slurred and lisping words the old man spoke.

"This speech is old, very old," said Kuran. "He asked why we have come down the road of the gods and what do we wish of him."

"Tell him that we seek to attack the pirates and that Watson told us of this route. We mean no harm to his people."

Haltingly the Moro translated. The chief looked from the three fronting him to the others waiting above before he answered.

"He says," interpreted Kuran, "that the evil ones have

many strange weapons and deal death in many wicked ways. Even brave men may rightly fear to face battle with them. But if we do not, then shall he show us the other end of the gods' old road for we must be those of whom the white man spoke, the men who bring fire and sword to cleanse this land."

"Tell him we'll take the gods' road," Sam called. "I'd like to see the Jap or Nazi who can face us down! We'll cleanse the land all right!"

17

OPERATION CAVEMAN

"**A**nd this passage takes us to the main cave held by the pirates? Ask him that again, Kuran, we must be sure," van Bleeker urged the Moro.

"He says that that is so. But there are many stones there — a wall which must be broken through — "

"I wonder — " Van Bleeker tapped his teeth with his thumbnail. "What about it, van Norreys? Could we use grenades? You know about such things."

"I would have to see the target before deciding that. No use bringing the roof down on our heads. But we must get into the principal cave first."

Old Toothless, somehow Watson's nickname stuck in spite of the dignity of the spare old man, had courage enough — though it was plain that he was no fighting man by choice. He not only guided them into the last stretch of the "road of the gods", but he insisted upon accompanying them.

Dust swirled out under their feet. It had been a long time since any but ghosts had passed this way. The bare

Walls gave way to a series of niches in each of which leered or postured a demon-headed godling. There was a glint of metal in the trappings they wore under a cloak of dust and bat droppings, and from their eye sockets glistened what could only be precious or semi-precious stones.

"Did someone mention treausre!" Sam whistled. "Looks as if we hit the jackpot in this robbers' den."

"Devils," the Moro leader spat in disdain. "Abominations in the Sight of Allah."

"In anybody's sight, I would say." Kane snapped his eyes away from a cruelly obscene figure. "If these are gods — what must their worshipers be?"

Toothless suddenly cut his pace from trot to walk and caught at the arms of the nearest two of the party, pulling them back as he mumbled a warning he had to repeat twice before Kuran could understand.

"He says that we are close now to the wall of many stones and that it would be well for us to go quietly, since he does not know whether sounds made here carry to the cave beyond."

They crept on, rounded a curve, and found themselves fronted by a mass of loose stones which looked to be the result of a cave-in. Lorens, Kane, and Sam ventured up to it, although the whole mass looked insecure enough to slide out and engulf them. Tentatively Sam poked at a sharp rock. To his surprise it remained as firmly fixed as if it had been set with cement. With more courage he pulled at another.

"Tight — "

Lorens was making his own investigations. "Yes. Explosives will be needed to start this."

Kane turned his torch up at the roof of the passage. Smoothed by man's work it ran without crack or blemish.

"What about it? Will this hold if we use a grenade?"

"If we use one of the special ones, I think so. At any rate we have no choice but to try."

The main party moved back around the curve to the comparative safety of the passage. Lorens' fingers closed once more about the familiar smoothness of a small grenade one of the *Sumba*'s men produced at van Bleeker's order. As he had many times before, he swung, threw, and dashed for cover, pressing his body against the floor of the passage.

But the sound of the explosion was oddly muffled and did not reverberate through the walls as they had thought it would. They edged forward, weapons in hand.

There was a break in the wall, showing murkily through the swirls of dust. Kane crawled up to it, fighting rolling stones. He coughed and choked in the dust and grit which clogged nose and throat. Then he looked through the hole into what Toothless said was the central headquarters of the cave-dwelling pirate forces.

The explosion had blown most of the barrier outward into the large cavern. And it must have come as an unnerving shock to the men gathered there. Watson had said that the cave dwellers had lights, but apparently the shock of the blast had put them out. Above the rattle of still falling stones there was no other sound. Then a beam of a flash, yellow and weak, sprouted by the far wall. Theirs answered, to catch and hold a small group of white-faced men.

One of the men in the light made a sudden movement. The crack of a rifle answered him, and he slid down to the floor, his face still a wild mask of horror and surprise.

"Achtung!" At the barked order the other two men instinctively came to attention. And, in answer to the stream of guttural syllables which followed, they turned their faces to the wall and stood with their hands high over their heads, pressed flat against the rock.

"Good!" Lorens ended in English, then added in

Malay, "Keep the light on them as we go down. At any move, shoot!"

Kane, Sam, Lorens, van Bleeker, and some others picked a cautious path over the rubble. Lorens and Kane swung their lights along the walls and found three exits to the cave. As soon as their torches picked these out, they held steady. There was going to be no chance of surprise.

In one corner they found a pile of boxes and matting-covered bundles. Against the wall nearby two rude bunks had been built. But that was all. And in due time their search brought them to the captives whom van Bleeker's men had been making into neat packages.

Quietly, almost disinterestedly, Lorens began questioning them in German. One of the men, a tall youngster, as stiff as steel and a willing martyr if Kane ever saw one, rapped out a single sentence in reply. Lorens smiled and shrugged.

"He says that they do not give information."

Kuran pressed forward. He was armed, but he made no parade of his weapons. Nor was there anything unpleasant in his calm face. But when he spoke Kane had little liking for the unholy promise in his voice.

"Let the Tuans give this eater of dirt to me. We shall speedily learn then whatever we wish."

Lorens laughed and the sardonic amusement which had brought that wolfish sound out of him was plain to read on his lips and in the upward quirk of his eyebrows.

"Quite appropriate," was his comment. "Well?" he spat at the captives.

The martyr did not answer, but his companion was fashioned of more malleable stuff. He gushed forth such a stream of information that Lorens was hard put to catch it all. Then at last the Netherlander nodded to a Moro standing behind the man and a brown hand was clapped expertly over the still babbling lips.

"Fortune favors us. This is the center stronghold, and

all the caves these swine are using can be reached by these passages. The majority of the Nazis and all the leading Japs are at sea — seems that our friends do not trust one another. This is the guard of the treasure chamber. They are to be relieved in about fifteen minutes. The Japs are not allowed in here at all. If we capture the relieving guard, we'll only have a dozen Japs and six more Nazis to pick up. Three of the Nazis are up in the crater watching our ships — "

"Who is in command here?" demanded van Bleeker.

Lorens pointed to the corpse against the wall. "Watson's 'Red Turban' is at sea. So I gather that the late unlamented was." He stopped to examine a badge on the worn coat which clothed the body. When he lifted his head again Kane saw his look of puzzlement.

"There is something familiar about this one — "

Van Bleeker crowded up to see for himself. He shook his head.

"Never saw him before. Just another Hun — "

"But I have seen him!" It was Sam's turn to take a second look and after a deliberate survey of the dead man's face he whistled.

"You know him?" Lorens asked.

"Not personally. But we hit the jackpot with this one, brother. That's Ludwig Baumer!"

"What?"

"Certain sure. His ugly face was on posters all over the place — in the papers too. This is the guy who was supposed to have skipped with all of Hitler's secret dope — the one who was never satisfactorily accounted for. Boy, oh, boy — have we done it, or have we done it!"

"So? Well, that we can discuss later. These two we shall put where they can do no more mischief and then we will take the other caves."

Under van Bleeker's orders the two captives, gagged lest they try the heroic role and attempt to warn the guard, were pushed into a niche behind some of the boxes they had been guarding and the invaders settled down to wait for the relief to arrive.

"What about the lights being out?" questioned Kane. "Won't they be suspicious about that?"

"I think not," Lorens answered him. "The lights must fail many times because of their faulty equipment. And I have a plan — "

They heard a sound then, the smack of boots against rock. Lorens called out in German, sharply as if giving an order. The answer came cheerily enough; apparently the newcomers had no premonition of danger.

"I have told them," Lorens whispered, "that there has been a fall of rock and that they must come carefully lest they trip over the debris. Also to come one at a time. Now — we take them!"

They allowed the guard to come into the cave. The light of the single torch the Nazis carried picked out the rubble of the barrier, and their voices arose in excited cries. But then those shadows which had been creeping between them and the entracne sprang. There was vast confusion for a moment or two in the dark before torches snapped on and tried to keep in their circles of light the three separate battles being waged on the floor.

Fortnight arose from one such struggle, leaving his opponent a limp bundle of torn clothes and flaccid limbs. "This one — " he reported to Kane apologetically — "I think that I hit him too hard — he is dead."

But the other two had breath enough remaining in their battered bodies for them to be stowed with the first catch and left there under guard.

"So far, so good." Sam wiped his hands on his slacks. "Does it strike you that all of this is a little too easy? I am going to walk softly the rest of the way — no use tempting fate."

A little judicious questioning of the new captives revealed that the enemy forces were more or less scattered. A Japanese ambush was in place along each of the two known trails by which one might descend from the crater. Of the remaining men, several snipers were posted in the jungle to pick off rash invaders, and the rest were in a sort of general outer headquarters for both Japanese and Nazis which was maintained in one of the three entrance caves.

The allied force split into three parties, leaving four of their men to guard prisoners and loot. Kane, Sam, and Lorens headed one, van Bleeker and a picked handful of seamen comprised the second, while the third was mostly Moro with Kuran and Fortnight at its head.

This last combination, trained jungle fighters that they were, volunteered to backtrack on the crater road and account for the ambush parties and any observation posts. Since they unslung their rifles and the two tommy guns they possessed and drew knives, Kane imagined that the toll of prisoners taken in their operation would be very few — if any.

The Moros filed off down through the tunnel almost lightheartedly. But Kuran was no novice. His brace of scouts glided on a good twenty feet ahead of the bulk of his force, and all of them had kicked off their sandals, to walk barefoot and noiselessly.

The task force commanded by van Bleeker was to attack the outer headquarters, knocking out that nerve center before it could rally a defense. Kane's group was to root out the snipers in the jungle. Not that they were expected to proceed on that mission without a guide. Lorens jerked to his feet the most talkative of their captives.

What the Netherlander muttered in the Nazi's ear must have been potent, for the German nodded vigorously and made whooing noises through his gag indicative of cordial agreement. But Lorens did not loosen either bonds or gag, instead he looped a piece of rope around the prisoner's neck and led him along as if the Nazi were a hound.

"What's the big idea?" Kane asked as their party turned into the third tunnel.

"When one hunts ducks, one uses a decoy. My decoy shall quack to some purpose — wait and see."

They met with no opposition in the passage or in the cave at the other end. Kane sniffed disgustedly at the fetid odor of the place where the bunks along the walls and the pile of cooking pots gave forth an aroma which was not exactly Chanel Number Five — as Sam was quick to point out.

"Looky here!" One of the seamen from the *Sumba* had chanced to peer into a tall earthen jar and was now staring down at its contents in startled amazement. With the toe of his shoe he sent it crashing, and Kane leaped to avoid the rush of water —

But things came with the water, long, black, slimy things, and Sam went back against a bunk with a smack which almost left him breathless. The nearest seaman brought his rifle butt down once, twice, and pursued a third wriggling length until it slipped out of reach into a crack.

"Snakes!"

Sam gagged. On his smooth skin the sweat made glistening beads. But he came back, forcing himself across the floor to the first of the broken but still writhing bodies. Only Kane could guess what it cost the Nisei to take that long look.

"Sea snakes." Sam's voice was harsh with effort. "The Japanese eat them."

His hand went to his mouth. But with a struggle which left him shaking he mastered his nausea.

"We're not hunting snakes!" Kane snapped. He caught Sam by the shoulder and pushed the smaller man ahead of him toward the outer air. "At least not the legless kind. Let's get back to work."

They looked out and down. Below were the trees of the jungle and the ragged open patches which marked the cultivated spaces. Lorens jerked the prisoner up and motioned along the jungle sweep with his hand. The Nazi answered with a gobbling noise, and Lorens had to cut the gag.

For several moments the man studied the terrain, then he pointed to four widely separated points and spoke in German. To all the questions Lorens asked he replied readily enough.

"Three are in trees, and the fourth, a German, is in that outcrop of rock. What is your opinion — " the Netherlander asked the Americans.

"The rock will be the easiest to take." Sam was alert again. "That guy won't be expecting any trouble from the rear. If we swing up along the mountain there, it will be as easy as picking off a tame rabbit. But the Japs in trees — those will be tougher."

"Then let us three take the men in the trees and leave the German in the rocks to the men here — "

"As the Tuan says," one of the Malay seamen agreed with Sam, "that is a task without effort."

"Uh-huh," grunted the snake hunter. "Don't worry. We'll git th' bugger! Right away — "

At Lorens' assenting nod, the three men from the *Sumba* left the cave, not with the carelessness Kane had feared, but as if they actually had some idea of what they were doing, taking cover where they could.

With Kane's help Lorens made their captive fast on one of the bunks. Sam kept to the mouth of the cave, as far from the snakes as he could edge.

"I'll take the one in the palm down by the lagoon," he announced as the others returned. "I've already figured out how to get there."

"And I want the one by the stream," chimed in Lorens.

"Look here! How come I'm not allowed to have a choice?" demanded Kane. "All right. I suppose it's a case of last come, last served. That leaves me the guy in the tree with the bunch of yellow flowers halfway up its trunk. Hmm — "

He adjusted the ship's glasses and began a detailed examination of as much of the tree as he could see. The bunch of yellow flowers, apparently some form of orchid, marked it plainly enough. But in its mass of leaves and branches he could see no sign of any sniper, which was not unusual — the hiding game was probably one in which the Japanese was very proficient.

"I hope our little friend gave us the right steer — "

"He knows what will happen to him if his information proves to be incorrect," Lorens answered cheerfully.

They stripped for action, putting aside any accouterments which might impede their crawl through the jungle. Then, with a mutual mutter of 'good luck', they took the plunge.

The moist heat closed in like an envelope as Kane descended into the green maw of vegetation. He went slowly, picking out the landmarks he had noted at the cave. Luckily this was jungle which had been already partially tamed by years of man's hacking. He found a trail running in the right direction and used it as a guide.

His goal, the tree with the yellow flowers, grew on the edge of a small clearing where two giant trees had crashed some time ago, taking with them vines and saplings to make an open space. Kane found cover in the brush behind one of the rotting, insect-eaten trunks and started his search for the tree-roosting sniper. Inch by inch, branch by branch, almost leaf by leaf, he examined the tree. Of course, the fellow might be perched on the other side, but he doubted that. Instinct would place any sniper on this side, with the tree between him and the direction from which he expected trouble.

The vicious flies had already found the American's hiding place, and he began to wonder how long he could stand their attacks without the counteroffensive of slaps. Of course, he could take the chance, show himself as bait and hope for a split-second shot —

From the east came a thin, high scream, a cry which almost jerked Kane from his kneeling position to certain exposure. But his eyes held to the tree. And he saw a telltale movement of the leafy mass. Now his Reising sang, sharply and expertly. The leaves shook convulsively, but there was no outcry. Instead something dropped, plopping dully on the thick leaf mold.

The American crept forward, still ready to give a second burst of fire. Play-acting was a regular move in this type of warfare, and to play dead and so draw your enemy to you was the easiest and oldest trick of all. But Kane won to the shadow under the tree without seeing a second move above. And there, half-buried in the thick muck, he found a rifle, the telescopic sighted weapon of a trained Japanese sniper.

It took several minutes of searching to locate the body hanging from a limb fork. The sniper was tied to his tree after the usual custom, but he was very dead.

Taking up the rifle, Kane started back. He was faintly aware, now that he had time to think about it, that he had heard other shots. Maybe their part in the island battle was already over.

18

DIVISION OF SPOIL

"Yoo-layyyy-whooo!"

Sam's raucous imitation of a yodel shattered the jungle, sending into flight some equally harsh-voiced birds and probably scaring the apes out of their wits. But it served to summon the expeditions back to the cave.

The assorted bag of prisoners was a small one. In addition to those they had captured in the inner cave they now held two Japanese, very much the worse for wear, and another Nordic superman. Kane had foreseen the operation of the Moro party correctly. When they returned they came alone.

Van Bleeker eyed the captives, now dragged into the open for examination, with marked disfavor.

"Unlucky, always am I unlucky," he spat out. "Now we must feed and nurse these swine until we can dump them into the arms of the proper authorities. Why does it always happen so to me?"

Kuran drew his hand across his throat in a graceful but very sinister gesture. But the captain of the *Sumba* shook his head. "No, we do not kill them. Why should we descend to their level? We take them back to be a headache for better men — that is the law."

Kuran's opinion of such a law was plain to read in his expression, but he made no verbal protest. And van Bleeker sent a man back to the *Sumba* with orders to bring one of the ship's boats around and pick up the prisoners. For the present they were pushed to the back of the cave and a guard placed over them. Then van Bleeker and Kuran turned briskly to the more congenial task of reckoning up the loot.

The headquarters cave yielded papers and a locked briefcase which Kane and Sam claimed, though Kuran had his doubts about turning over the briefcase until the Americans pointed out that their interest in the loot would stop with that portion of the spoil. Their claim in the name of the United States might be high-handed and illegal, but they intended to hold to it.

The bales of goods taken from the inner cave were cargoes from the pirated ships. Much of it Kuran appeared to recognize, though Kane privately wondered if the Moro's pious claims were as true as they sounded. It was so easy to hail goods as one's own when there were no embarrassing shipping tags in evidence to prove one a liar.

But in a niche of the inner cave was a steel box which van Bleeker and Kuran both hammered at in turn until they forced it open to spill out its contents on the canvas cover of the nearest bale.

Kane had read of the fairy tale 'king's ransom' in jewels. But outside of the display of crown gems in the Tower of London, he did not believe that there ever had been such a treasure gathered in one place before. It was a tangle of brilliant fire.

Even Kuran blinked and, from the men circled about

the leaders, came little murmurs and cries. Lorens' eyes narrowed. His hand gathered up a necklace of crystallized rainbow, and he held it closer to his eyes.

"You look as if you know that one," Kane said.

"Perhaps I do. It is European in design. And so is this, and this — " He pushed aside a tiara, several rings, a wide bracelet of sullen crimson squares. "But these" — he separated from the lot some bulky pieces of far different workmanship — "are Eastern." He glanced at old Toothless who was as big-eyed as the rest. "Ask him — are these from his people?"

When Kuran had translated that question the old chief cackled a long sentence or two which excited the Moro. But the old man made no move toward the display of gems; in fact he backed away a little from the bale where they rested.

"He says that these must be from the treasure storehouse of the wicked Rajah — he whose sins brought evil to this island many years ago. And so these are cursed, and it will be ill for any man to take them — even as it was ill for the pirates. For ever since they broke into the burial place of the Rajah and looted these they have quarreled amongst themselves, and several have been slain. He suggests that it would be wise to throw these into the sea lest the curse fall also upon us — "

Lorens had been working swiftly while Kuran spoke, sorting the jewels into two piles. Those of oriental style in one, and those from Europe in the other.

"Well," he said to the Moro, "do you agree that these are accursed?" He pushed the pile of stones toward Hakroun's son, but the man made no move to reach for them.

"There are things which bear with them the Curse of Allah. And a wise man does not meddle with such. Let one braver than I provoke the Jinns of outer space!"

"You, van Bleeker?"

But the captain of the *Sumba* did not put out his hand either. He laughed, and the sound was one of embarrassment. "My living depends upon the good will of native peoples. I would not dare go against their beliefs — not even for a Rajah's treasure!"

Kane looked at the jewels. "Why not," he began somewhat shyly, then continued with more assurance, "why not sell them and give the money to Toothless? After all, these belonged to his people a long time ago. And maybe some witch doctor can take the spell off them — as the captain had that curse taken off the *Sumba* at Jolo."

"And what do you say to that?" Lorens spoke not to the leaders now but to the outer circle of seamen and Moros.

Eurasian, Moro, Malay, Kanaka, Javanese, and European, they shuffled their feet, grinned, or just shook their heads firmly. They wished none of such ill-omened loot. It was the bosun of the *Sumba*, the snake hunter, who voiced their general opinion.

"There's enough o' this here other stuff. No use muckin' around wi' these here curses. They's funny stuff — I've seen 'em act. I'm votin' wi' Mr. Kane. Let these island Johnnies have th' dough. It's their junk, ain't it?"

"Boat comin', sir!" The call came from the cave entrance to put an end to the discussion.

Lorens bundled all the jewels back into the box and kept the case under his arms as they went out. The boat had arrived all right, they could see it nosing in to the beach. And there seemed to be an unusually large number of people crowded into her. They didn't come directly up from the beach either, but milled around down there on the scrap of sand as if engaged in assembling something. And, when they did start up the path the pirates had worn, Kane saw that bearers trotted along with two occupied hammocks swung between them.

Kuran permitted himself a slight smile and waved a

hand toward the cortege.

"It is my father. The old one must see for himself what we do. Last night it was necessary to argue much against his coming. This time — when I am not there to speak, he gives his own orders. So now he comes!"

Abdul Hakroun did occupy the first hammock. And behind him in the second rode Watson. Apparently the gunner was determined not to be left out. The old Moro held himself as erect as he could in his swinging cradle, his hands gripping the fiber rope edges of his conveyance desperately. And his cries of admonition began to reach the party at the caves.

But when, a short time later, he had been established in full dignity again on a couch made of the cleanest coverings from the bunks, he was as serene as ever. He greeted the warriors graciously and waited for a full battle report from his son.

Kane dropped down beside Sam and Watson.

"I was just telling the sergeant here that we haven't had a chance yet to look for his buddy's stuff," said Sam under the cover of Kuran's story.

"He had a class ring — I'd like to send that back to his folks. The rest of the stuff — that we took from the other boys — is hidden back in the caves. Toothless knows where."

"Listen," Kane interrupted. "Suppose you tell us more about your crash. That was what we were really sent out here for, Sam and I, to hunt planes which had disappeared in these parts during the war and see if there were any survivors. So give us the works — "

"You were? Great guns, the war must really be over if they're starting to look for us missing guys! That's swell! Our plane was the Vigilante — "

"Capt. Rodney Safield, pilot," cut in Sam. "So this is it, Dutch, the end of our trail — "

"He means," Kane explained to the bewildered

Watson, "that we were sent after your plane. You see, Safield's father is a millionaire, and he thought his son might still be alive. He's backing this little jaunt of ours."

"The captain got his when the Jap flak clipped our wings. He never knew what hit us. Jerry Conway, he was co-pilot, nursed her along. We thought we might have a better chance over the little islands than where the Japs were so plentiful. They must'a got Jack Kaproski with the same burst which knocked off the captain. Jack was bombardier.

"Anyway, we limped along, Jerry nursing her. She was a gone goose, though, and we knew we didn't have a chance of getting back. So when we sighted this island and we couldn't see any signs of Japs, Jerry ordered us to hit silk. Well, Pete got away, and I did, and so did Dan, he was a waist gunner.

"But Larch, our navigator, got fouled up some way and was dragged down with her, and I guess Jerry didn't try at all. We never did find out what happened to the other guys.

"She came straight in to the lagoon, and I thought she was going to smack into the mountain. But she didn't — it was queer, she dug into the water, ramming her nose right into the reef. We got ashore somehow, lucky we three could swim. And Pete did some diving so in a couple of days we got Jerry and the captain out and buried them. The captain's papers are hid with our stuff. And Pete wrote out a sort of report we all signed so — well, so if we weren't ever found 'til too late somebody might learn what had happened to us. He sealed everything up and made old Toothless and all his principal men swear they'd give it to the first man who came looking for us — if one ever did."

"The only thing I don't understand," said Kane, "is what you were doing on the Vigilante. We were given a full list of the crew, and there's no Sgt. Tucker Watson on it."

Watson grinned ruefully. "That's just luck — don't know whether to say good or bad. I changed with Shorty Dulesberg at the last minute. I was a replacement, see. Our ship, the Fighting Polecat, washed out after the last run. Boy, she was nothing but lace work; you could have thrown an elephant right through her — easy. So while we sat around waiting to see if they could patch her up again, we substituted for guys in the other crates. Shorty had a bad eye, lid cut or something, and I went in for him. I didn't know any of the guys very well then — 'course afterwards, well, Dan, Pete, and me got to know each other all right. I can even tell you what Dan had to eat for his birthday party the year he was ten — Yeah, we sure got to know each other then. So that's why I wasn't on your list."

"Kane, Marusaki!" Lorens was hailing them. Reluctantly the two Americans joined the other group in time to hear van Bleeker say, "So already the government is cutting in? Very well, let them take the prisoners — as for this loot — perhaps the laws of salvage may apply — "

Abdul Hakroun laughed. "Oh, there will be some compensation for our efforts, my friend, never fear. Does not your own 'Book of Books' say that 'the laborer is worthy of his hire'?"

"What's up?" Kane asked Lorens.

"A radio message has come from Besi — a destroyer put in there and heard our earlier message. She is sailing to us now."

"She'll be useful for rounding up pirate ships homeward bound," Sam pointed out. "Only I foresee a lot of snooping around and questions being asked. Somehow I don't think that these little private wars are welcomed by the authorities. Also, what about that collection of sparklers you're nursing? Aren't they part of the loot?"

"The best part, perhaps. The European pieces were

probably a collection made by the Nazis for future insurance. It must go back to Europe where it can be identified. And what about those papers you were so quick to impound?"

Kane grinned. "Oh, we have someone who will be only too, too pleased to receive them as a coming-home present. This sort of thing is his favorite reading matter."

"You'd better prepare to face a battle over them," Sam cut in. "The red tape artists all like to prove that they can read. Only, I don't want to face old Ironjaw without some little token of my esteem. His feelings are apt to be hurt — he's rather touchy."

Abdul Hakroun was inspecting the loot with a jealous eye, his Moros unpacking box and bale to view their contents. The *Sumba*'s men drifted unostentatiously off on side expeditions of their own which no one was untactful enough to question. So it came about that there were just Hakroun, van Bleeker, Lorens, and the Americans gathered in the cave. The Moro leader glanced around before he spoke in a low voice.

"I am a man of business, Capt. van Bleeker. And soon, when our naval friends arrive, we shall be occupied by great affairs and will have no time to speak of such matters. Therefore let us now deal with the problem of the pearl beds — "

Van Bleeker struck a match to light a cigarette. His eyes were half closed, he had a lazy contented look about him. Only Kane, having seen him at trading before, mistrusted that pose.

"You propose?" The captain of the *Sumba* was almost indifferent.

"I propose to found a company to work together as good friends — even as we fought together to clear this place of stinking vermin. I have the divers to pluck the beds, you have an excellent supply ship, and you, Tuan," the Moro nodded to Lorens, "have a place in the market in which we must sell our wares. So let us work as one — we are all honest men." His eyes held laughter, and Lorens' smile answered it.

"I have heard many things of you, Abdul Hakroun," the Netherlander returned frankly. "But also I have been told that if you once give your word you hold to it against all the world."

Hakroun tugged at his beard. "A merchant hopes for a bargain — that is his due. But between friends there is no bargain. Shall I swear it upon the Word of the Prophet?"

The two Netherlanders exchanged a swift glance. Van Bleeker snapped the ash off his cigarette.

"Three ways we divide?" he asked.

"If you wish. But there is the custom of your own people. Why not divide into many pieces — stock as you would call it."

Sam chuckled. "Stock in a pearl bed? How about it, Watson? That sound good to you?"

"Let it be that way." Van Bleeker ground out his cigarette. "We split the stock three ways, and each then decides who he will share with."

"But it does not go beyond this present company!" Hakroun warned.

"That is understood," Lorens agreed. "Let us have a hundred shares. One to go to the head of these cave people, thirty-three to each of us. Then — "

"Not more than five altogether for us — how about it, boys?" Kane asked his countrymen.

"Okay. After all, we more or less came along for the ride," Sam returned.

"Geez!" Watson pulled himself up. "Do I rate an in on this too?"

"Well, you found Capt. van Bleeker's back door for him," Kane reminded him.

The captain of the *Sumba* had been writing on a page torn from his pocket notebook and now he made a copy of his work and passed them both around the group for signatures. One he kept, and one he handed to Hakroun.

"How soon does the business start humming?" Sam wanted to know.

"Tomorrow — or after the government ship has gone," Hakroun answered. "My divers are aboard my ship. Already they look for a place to build their village here — "

"All's well that ends well — or has that been said before?" Sam stretched his arms wide over his head. "Just think, brother, we're now regular, dyed-in-the-wool — or maybe soaked-in-the-water — pearl fishermen. Wonder what Ironjaw will have to comment on that. Of course, there was absolutely nothing said in San Francisco against side line projects — "

"If we put this on his desk he'll forget all about us." Kane picked up the briefcase. "And if, before we face out of his life, we are able to offer him Baumer on toast he may even love us — "

Sam managed a very realistic shudder of abhorrence. "What a beastly idea. But I don't doubt that there will be dancing and feasting the halls occupied by the High Intelligence when we are able to report. Only then we shall be the forgotten men."

"Well, then we can come back here and be stock-holders protecting our interests. How about it, Lorens, can you use a couple of good inside or outside men? We can bring testimonials — I think."

"Whenever you wish to come, you shall be welcome — and there will be work to do."

Kane sobered. "D'you know, I think that you mean that!"

"But naturally. Do you think that this affair is the end of all our journeying? No, we are but beginning. For you there can be beginnings too."

"That we shall keep in mind — for reference if Ironjaw

is not in the best of moods." Sam caught up the offer with his usual lightness. "What about you, Watson? Does Stateside have any appeal?"

"Does it!" The light which came into the thin face of the gunner made the force of his answer double. "Lordy, fellas, when do we sail?"

"After the red tape merchants have had their way with us probably. You know" — Sam ran his fingers through the thick waves of his hair — "there's only one loose end which we can't tuck neatly into the pattern."

"And that?" asked Kane.

"What were those Johnnies looking for — the ones who made hay of our stuff back in Manila?"

"The answer to that quiz question is easy." Kane slung his gun over his shoulder and tied the briefcase to his belt with his handkerchief. "They were probably looking for two other guys — "

ANDRE NORTON

Born in 1912, Alice Mary Norton writing under the pseudonym of Andre Norton has become one of the world's bestselling author's. Although she began her career by writing adventure and historical novels in the 1930's, Ms. Norton turned to science fiction in the 1950's and it is in that genre that she has made her most significant contribution. She is generally regarded as one of the foremost writers of "space opera", and is certainly one of the best-selling women authors in the field.

As a teenager Ms. Norton planned a career as a history teacher; she eventually became a children's librarian and a professional writer. Both her early interest in history and her library training in research have played significant roles in her writing. Norton extensively researches each of her books, using folklore, legends, history (especially Greek and Roman), archeology, anthropology, and the occult in her fiction. Her careful scholarship is evident in her work, which is frequently praised for its convincing backgrounds. Norton's first novel, *The Prince Commands*, was accepted for publication before she was 21. She continued to write historical fiction until the 1940's, when she turned to adventure and spy stories. An espionage novel, *THE SWORD IS DRAWN*, was given an award by the Netherlands government in 1946 for its portrayal of that nation at war.

Although she had been writing science fiction sporadically for some time, it was only after she had edited several science fiction anthologies that Norton found a publisher for her first science fiction novel, *Star Man's Son*. The success of this book and Norton's subsequent titles helped open the field for other writers.

She now resides in Winter Park, Florida.